For Mark and Jeremy, my two favourite nephews,*
with megatons of love from Auntie Vegg

* I only have two

Acknowledgements

With thanks again to Sarah Dudman, my supersplendiferous editor, whose advice and suggestions are invaluable, and to Nina Charlton at Eastbourne Central Library who helps me with research.

Norman Longmate's book *The Workhouse*, Jonathon Green's *Dictionary of Slang* and *The London Encyclopaedia*, edited by Ben Weinreb and Christopher Hibbert, were great sources of information. And what would I do without dear old Henry Mayhew . . . ?

Jammy Dodgers go Underground

Also by Bowering Sivers

Jammy Dodgers on the Run

Jammy Dodgers go Underground

BOWERING SIVERS

MACMILLAN CHILDREN'S BOOKS

First published 2005 by Macmillan Children's Books
a division of Macmillan Publishers Ltd
20 New Wharf Road, London N1 9RR
Basingstoke and Oxford
www.panmacmillan.com

Associated companies throughout the world

ISBN 1 405 04580 9

1 3 5 7 9 8 6 4 2

A CIP catalogue record for this book is available from
the British Library.

Typeset by Intype Libra Ltd
Printed and bound in Great Britain by Mackays of Chatham plc, Kent

Contents

1

Ma Perkinski plodded into the yard at Devil's Acre late one hot summer's night carrying a heavy sack.

'What've you got in there, Ma?' Her three sons gathered round her eagerly as she heaved it off her shoulder with a sigh of relief.

'It's a surprise.'

'Is it squibs and crackers?' asked Ned.

'Squibs and crackers? Don't be soft, son, it isn't Guy Faux night. Besides, why would I waste good money on fireworks?'

'Is it grub?' asked Billy, drooling at the thought of a sackful of pork pies.

'You'll have to wait till the mornin' to find out,' said Ma, pushing them away. 'I'm too done up now.'

Jem, Ned and Billy spent a restless night wondering what the surprise was and several times their sister Kate told them to stop whispering – 'Or I'll stick the three of you in the varminty sack and chuck you in the river!'

In the morning they watched with mounting excitement as Ma untied the sack and tipped it upside down. A pile of dirty boots tumbled on to the dusty ground – Wellingtons and Napoleons and Hessians, half-boots known as 'highlows', boots with elastic sides, boots with eyelets, boots with buttons, all of them so well worn they were in imminent danger of falling apart.

'Oh crikey,' said Jem, looking at them with a glum expression. 'Trotter cases.'

'What a crummy surprise,' grumbled Ned. And Billy, who had dreamed about pork pies all night long, began to snivel.

'I got the whole lot for sixpence at the Monmouth Street market,' said Ma, well pleased with herself.

'Huh, you got a real bargain there, Ma,' said Jem, picking one up. 'I always wanted a boot that let in lots of fresh air,' he sniggered, poking his fingers through a large hole in the sole.

'None of your lip. It's better than what you're wearin',' she scolded him. 'Now stop glumpin', the lot of you. Go on, Ned, you too, Billy, choose a pair and I'll sell the rest.'

But choosing a pair was impossible because none of the boots matched.

'They don't have to look the same,' said Ma, 'long as they fit you, more or less. Try these on, Ned.'

'The left one does, Ma, but the right one's too tight.'

'Here, let me have a go,' she said. And kneeling down, she pushed against the boot with all her might.

'Aargh!' yelled Ned. 'You're squashin' my toes. They gone dead.'

'Jem, run in the caravan and get Pa's knife. I'll cut the top off this boot and it'll fit Ned right as ninepence. Now what about you, Billy?' Ma turned to the little boy.

'They're all too big for me.'

'Well, that's all to the good, son, cos you'll grow into them. Put these on.'

'But they're both left feet, Ma.'

'Oh, for Lor's sake, you can bend your right foot till it fits. Now put them boots on and hook it,' she exclaimed, shooing the boys out of the yard like a flock of geese. 'And don't come back till you've earned some money, d'you hear, else there'll be no supper for you tonight.'

★

'So what'll we do?' said Jem, as the three of them trudged out of Devil's Acre.

'We could sell watercresses,' suggested Ned. 'People eat a lot of watercresses in hot weather.'

'Cor, that's a stunnin' idea, Ned. How much watercresses you got to sell?'

'I haven't got none. But we could buy some.'

'Oh yeh? What with?'

'All right, all right.' Ned scowled. 'I was just tryin' to be helpful.'

'We could swallow snakes,' said Billy.

'What?' His two brothers stared at him aghast.

'I saw a bloke when we went to that fair in Greenwich. People were givin' him loads of money for swallowin' snakes – stunnin' big ones too.'

'They can't've been that big, else he couldn't have swallowed them.' Jem shook his head doubtfully.

'How big were they, Billy?' asked Ned.

'Like that.' Billy held his hands about ten inches apart.

'They weren't snakes, they must've been worms,' scoffed Jem.

'They were snakes. *They were.* The bloke said so.'

'So how'd he swallow them?'

'He put one in his mouth and held its tail and

then he pinched it and it stuck its head and shoulders down his throat.'

'A snake hasn't got no shoulders.'

'Dry up, Ned,' said Jem. 'And what happened when the bloke swallowed it, Billy?'

'He didn't. He said you got to hold on to its tail real tight so it doesn't go right down into your belly. I wonder what snakes taste like.' The little boy licked his lips thoughtfully.

'I don't know and I'm not intendin' to find out,' said Jem. 'Let's go to the Square and see if we can pick up cigar-ends. Old man Roberts'll give us sixpence a pound for them. Come on, Billy,' he urged the little boy, who was dawdling along behind them. 'What's wrong with you? Why're you goin' round in circles?'

'It's my new boots, Jem,' he whined.

'What's wrong with them?'

'They're both left-footers. I can't hardly walk straight.'

'Well, take one off then. We're bound to find some mug who'll buy it.'

2

The whole country was writhing in the fiery grip of a heatwave. Day after day the sun rose in the east and trundled across the cloudless sky like a mobile furnace, scorching everyone and everything in its path.

Wealthy Londoners, aristocrats and merchants who lived in Mayfair and Regent's Park, closed up their houses and set off for their estates in the country. The not-quite-so-wealthy, who lived on the edge of the capital in rural retreats like Finchley or Dulwich, sat in their gardens under the trees sipping lemonade brought to them by their servants.

But there were others, many others, not so fortunate. Too poor, too sick, too old or helpless to escape, packed into slum houses, ten, often twenty, to a room, they had no choice but to suffer the stifling heat of the city.

By day they sweated, toiling up and down

crowded streets with heavy trays suspended from their necks loaded with an assortment of useful and useless items, from rat poisons and flypapers to fans and fireworks. Others scoured the foul-smelling sewers for pieces of iron, copper nails and bits of rope or searched dustbins for old rags – anything, in short, they could sell to buy a little food and a night's lodging.

The onset of darkness brought no relief. Tossing and turning on straw mattresses or hard floors, tormented by legions of fleas, lice and bedbugs, their uneasy slumber was constantly disturbed by noisy arguments in the streets below or the raucous, tuneless singing of a drunkard staggering back to his lodgings.

The three brothers were as weary as all the others they passed that morning, for they too had spent a sleepless night in the hot, cramped caravan they shared with their parents and their sister, Kate. They shuffled through the narrow, crowded streets behind Westminster Abbey, past 10 Downing Street where the Prime Minister was enjoying a hearty breakfast of boiled eggs, omelettes, bacon, chops and kidneys, past the Horse Guards barracks where tight-lipped sentries gazed determinedly into space, and into Trafalgar Square.

There, despite the heat and earliness of the hour, all was bustle and confusion. Horse-drawn buses and hansom cabs vied for space with a multitude of carriages, carts and wagons. Street urchins, many of them barefoot, barged into elegant gentlemen in top hats and frock coats. Young clerks on their way to work ogled pretty young women in lace-trimmed bonnets and long, full skirts with frills and flounces. Pickpockets darted among the crowd looking for a wallet or silk handkerchief to steal. Girls carrying baskets of fruit and flowers sang out their wares – 'Eight for a penny, juicy apples!' 'Lavender, sweet lavender!' 'Watercresses, all fresh and green!'

'Hey up, here comes a choker,' Ned said, as a sombre man in stovepipe hat and black suit approached them, swinging his cane. 'Wager you can't get nothin' out of him.'

'Wager I can,' said Jem with his usual confidence. 'I can always squeeze somethin' out of blokes in dog collars.' And going up to the clergyman, he swept off his hat, bowed low and said, 'Please, Your Holiness, could you help three poor little orphans that haven't got no mother nor father.'

The man stopped and frowned. 'Orphans do not have mothers and fathers. That is why they are called orphans,' he said curtly. 'It appears to me that you are begging for money. And begging is against the law. If I were to call a policeman . . .'

'Nah, nah, we're not beggin', Your Reverendness,' said Jem quickly. 'We're . . . er . . . we're sellin' . . . er . . . boots. Billy, show him yours.'

'One boot?' sniffed the clergyman as Billy held it up.

'You can have it for a penny, Your Goodness, or both of them for a penny ha'penny. Billy, take the other one off and—'

'No, thank you. I have no desire to buy two left boots, especially in such a disreputable condition. But to show that I am a gentleman of a generous disposition, here —' the clergyman pressed a farthing into Jem's hand — 'take this. Good day to you.' And with a smug expression on his face he strode away.

'A whole farthin'!' sniggered Ned. 'You certainly cleaned him out.'

'All right, all right, I only just started. I haven't got warmed up yet,' protested Jem. 'Billy, you look for cigar-ends while Ned and me do a bit of blobbin'.'

So, while Billy ran round the Square, his eyes glued to the pavement, searching for cigar butts, his brothers pestered people with hard-luck stories that should have brought tears to their eyes and coins from their pockets. But the citizens of London were too mean or too hot that day to be bothered with yet more ragged urchins importuning them and they brushed the boys aside with a scowl or curse.

Just before midday, when Jem had almost convinced a woman that he and Ned were dying of the plague and if she didn't give them a penny they'd collapse on the spot, there was a commotion on the other side of the Square.

'Whatever's happening?' cried the woman. And drawing up the strings of her purse she ran to see.

'Just our luck,' muttered Ned. 'It's probably just a soaker that's fallen under a horse.'

'Nah, it isn't a drunk — it's Billy. I can hear him bawlin' his head off,' said Jem. 'Come on plaguy quick, before a crusher gets there.'

But a policeman had already arrived. He was looking sternly at Billy and listening to a well-dressed man who said, 'He wants my cigar-end. I keep telling him I've only just lit it. Look.' He held up a large Havana with an impressive gold band around its middle.

'Ah,' nodded the crowd who had gathered to

watch, for they knew an expensive cigar when they saw one.

'It will take at least half an hour to smoke it, but this wretched child won't leave me alone,' said the man, trying in vain to shake off the little boy who clung to his arm like a limpet.

'Now then, young'un,' said the policeman, bending down to look Billy in the eye. 'You know what'll happen if you go on making a nuisance of yourself, don't you?'

'Yeh, I'll get the cigar.'

'No, you will not. You'll end up before the magistrate, my lad, and he'll send you to prison. Now, what do you think of that?'

'Will I get somethin' to eat there?'

'Course you will. We don't starve people in Her Majesty's prisons.'

'All right.' Billy let go of the cigar smoker's arm. 'You can put the bracelets on me,' he said, holding out his wrists to be handcuffed.

The crowd roared with laughter, but the policeman looked perplexed. 'You're a rum'un and no mistake,' he said, frowning.

'He doesn't mean it, guv. He doesn't rightly know what he's sayin',' said Jem, pushing his way to the front of the crowd. 'He's got apartments to let, if you get my meanin',' he said, tapping his head and rolling his eyes like a madman.

'How sad,' murmured someone.

'It's cos he's starvin',' explained Jem, taking advantage of the wave of compassion that was beginning to sweep through the crowd. 'His brain's kind of slid down into his belly cos it's so empty. Trouble is –' Jem wiped an imaginary tear from his eye – 'we haven't got the ready to buy him grub so he'll just have to die.' And he took off his wideawake and held it out.

Within minutes it was full of farthings, half-pennies and pennies. Even the man with the cigar put in a few coins – 'And you can have my cigar too,' he said, to the cheers and applause of the crowd.

3

'Very nice,' said Pa that evening, sitting on the steps of their caravan and inhaling the Havana's rich, pungent smoke. 'Real jammy. Best cigar I ever smoked. Matter of fact,' he chuckled, 'it's the only cigar I ever smoked.'

'And they made a shillin' as well,' said Ma approvingly.

'Nah, we made more than that,' piped up Billy. 'We made—'

'A shillin', like Ma said,' said Jem, twisting his brother's arm up his back to keep him quiet, for they had spent fourpence on hot potatoes, mutton pies and jam tarts, which they'd eaten sitting cross-legged on the pavement before going home to a supper of watery soup and dry bread.

'You should do that dodge again, Jem,' said Pa, finishing his cigar with a sigh of contentment. 'It's crushin'.'

*

The boys were back in Trafalgar Square early the next day. Billy had been instructed to look for the richest man he could find smoking a cigar – 'Cos he might give you the whole box,' said Pa, hopefully – and Jem had perfected his patter, even adding a heart-breaking description of the little coffin his father had made out of orange boxes for Billy when he finally departed this world. But there was a different policeman in the Square that morning and he informed Billy that if he didn't stop pestering people he would be taken away and given twenty lashes with a birch rod.

'And will I get somethin' to eat afterwards?' asked Billy.

'No, you will not,' retorted the policeman. 'You'll get another twenty lashes for being a sauce-box.'

'So we can't do that dodge no more,' sighed Jem, dragging Billy away. 'Now we got to think of somethin' else to do. Hey, what about that?' He pointed to a boy wielding a broom.

Ned turned to look. 'What – sweepin' crossin's? Nah, there's no money in it.'

'There is. That gent just gave him a coin. I reckon we could make a tidy sum.'

There were thousands of horses in London –

heavy beasts with shaggy manes and legs like tree trunks hauling carts piled high with beer barrels, glossy thoroughbreds drawing elegant carriages, their tails tied up with ribbons, sad old hacks with rheumy eyes and scabby hocks pulling hansom cabs and growlers. But whatever their differences they all had one thing in common – they dropped dung on the road, thousands of tons of it every day, alongside large pools of smelly pee and wads of hay that fell from their nosebags.

In bad weather the roads became even worse. Very few were paved with cobblestones and the rain churned the dirt and dust into a sea of mud. Although orderlies employed by the borough councils did their best to keep the streets clean, it was an impossible task. But necessity is the mother of invention. And the necessity for men in patent-leather buttoned boots and women in bootees of softest white kid to walk from one side of the road to the other without getting too covered in dust, mud and manure led to the invention of crossing sweepers.

Every main thoroughfare and square had its resi-dent crossing sweepers – poor, frequently poverty-stricken men, women and children who risked their lives diving in and out of the traffic to clear a path in return for a small tip.

'We couldn't do it, anyway,' said Ned. 'We haven't got no broom.'

'We could get one,' said Jem.

'Don't be barmy, they cost twopence ha'penny.'

'I said we'd *get* one, not buy one.'

'Nick it, you mean?'

'Borrow it.'

'Oh yeh? Not from him, we won't.' Ned nodded at the boy busily brushing a path outside the National Gallery, a tall, well-built youth with a face like a constipated bulldog. 'He'd more like flatten us with it.'

'Yeh, but what about her?' Jem pointed to a girl standing at a crossing near the church of St Martin-in-the-Fields.

Ned nodded. 'All right,' he said. 'Let's see you do it.'

'Hey, you!' Jem called out, running up to her. 'Your name Ellen?'

She squinted at him, her little button eyes full of suspicion. 'Nah. It's Clara.'

'Oh yeh, I remember now. Clara, your ma says you got to get home plaguy quick.'

'Why?'

'Cos your pa's had a accident.'

'I haven't got no pa.'

'I meant your uncle.'

'What, Uncle Bob?'

'Yeh, that's the one.'

'What's happened to him?'

'He got run over by a omnibus.'

'What, on a boat?'

'Nah, on the street.'

'Don't be a stupe – my uncle Bob's a sailor. He's been at sea this past six months.'

'Oh. Well, it must've been your brother then.'

'Not Pip?'

'Yeh, Pip.'

'Why didn't you say so in the first place, you numbskull?' the girl cried, starting to run.

'Oy!' Jem shouted after her.

'What?'

'Leave me your broom. I'll clean your crossin' for you.'

She narrowed her eyes at him. 'You got to give me half what you get.'

'Course I will.'

'Promise?'

'"Ain't this wet? Ain't this dry? Cut my throat if

 17

I tell a lie,'" chanted Jem, crossing his fingers behind his back.

'All right.' She handed him her broom and ran off.

'I hope you two were watchin' real close –' Jem turned to his brothers with a smug grin – 'on account of you've just seen a crack pro on the job. I got this off her smooth as cream,' he chortled, planting Clara's broom on the ground and doing a little jig around it.

Ned watched him with a jaundiced eye. 'Now let's see you get the ready off people *smooth as cream*,' he said.

'Me?' Jem stopped dancing and glared at his brother. 'I'm not doin' it. It's your turn.'

'What d'you mean, my turn?'

'I got the broom for us, didn't I?' said Jem indignantly. 'Why should I do all the pesky work?'

Muttering and scowling, Ned took the broom and stood on the edge of the pavement while Jem and Billy sat in the gutter watching. But though he scuttled back and forth across the road for an hour or more cleaning the crossing nobody gave him any money.

'Not much good at it, are you?' scoffed Jem.

'Ma'll give your backside a wallop with that broom if you go home empty-handed.'

'See if you can do any better then,' said Ned, throwing the broom at him.

'Course I can. I'll show you how it's done . . . Sweep the crossin' for you, missus?' said Jem, running up to an elderly woman who was about to step off the pavement.

'Where's the little girl who is usually here?'

'She's dead.'

'Clara is *dead*?' The woman stopped and looked at Jem in horror. 'The poor child. How did it happen?'

'She was hit by lightnin'. Burned to a crisp. Nothin' left but the buttons on her dress.'

'How dreadful.' The woman's eyes filled with tears.

'Yeh, it is,' agreed Jem. 'We're collectin' for her funeral.' He took off his wideawake and held it out. 'Sixpence'll do – or a shillin', if you can spare it.'

'And who are you?'

'I'm her brother Pip.'

The woman stopped dabbing her eyes with a lace-edged handkerchief and glared at Jem. '*You* are Pip?'

'Yeh, that's right.'

19

'Clara brings Pip here when her mother is unwell. He's barely a year old.'

'Ah . . . Yeh . . . Well, you see, that's *Little* Pip. I'm . . . er . . . I'm her other brother, *Big* Pip.'

'You're a big liar, that's what you are,' exclaimed the woman. And brushing him aside angrily, she walked away.

'Hey, that was stunnin', Jem,' said Ned, laughing fit to bust. 'You're a crack pro and no kid.'

'Shut your pan!' growled Jem, swinging the broom back, but it was twisted out of his hands before it connected with his brother's head.

'Oy, what d'you think you're doin'?' he shouted, spinning round.

'Just what I was goin' to ask you,' said the boy with the face like a bulldog, waving the broom menacingly. 'We been watchin' you, haven't we?' he said to the other crossing sweepers who had gathered around him.

'Yeh, we have, Captain. He cut up Clara, we saw him. Stole her broom he did and sent her packin'.'

'Right, there's nothin' for it, he'll have to come before the court.'

'Him and the other one,' said a red-haired girl, pointing at Ned.

'I wasn't doin' nothin' wrong,' protested Ned. 'I'm not goin' to no court.' And he turned to run.

'Grab him,' said the boy called Captain. 'Him too.' He gestured at Jem, who was laying about him with fists and feet. And a dozen hands reached out and frogmarched the two brothers down the street while Billy ran along behind, bawling his head off.

'Him with you?' said Captain.

'He's my brother,' snarled Jem, red in the face from struggling. 'Don't touch him or I'll—'

'Stash it, littl'un, or I'll give your backside such a tannin' you'll never sit down again,' said Captain, sweeping Billy off his feet and tucking him under his arm.

4

Pa Perkinski was leaning against a stall in Covent Garden, drinking coffee from a tin and eating a slice of buttered bread as thick as a brick.

'Market's busy today, Bert,' said a porter, tossing one of his empty baskets upside down on the ground and lowering himself on to it with a sigh of relief. 'The strawberry season always brings them in. I've heard say there are four or five thousand here.'

'I reckon you can double that, Bill,' said Pa. 'If you ask me, everyone in London's here.'

'You still boxin', Bert?' enquired the stallholder, cleaning a chipped plate with a dirty rag.

'Nah, I haven't had a fight in months, not a proper one, not like they used to be. Them London Prize Ring Rules've spoilt it, if you ask me. We're not allowed to kick or headbutt our hopponents. We can't even bite their ears off or gouge their eyes out. Nah, it's not a sport no more. And there's no

money in it neither, not like there used to be . . .
Well, I can't stand here clackin' all day,' Pa said,
ramming the rest of the bread in his mouth and
swilling it down with the remains of the coffee. 'See
you tomorrow then, Kev.' And he put a penny on
the counter.

'Er . . . that'll be twopence, Bert,' said the stallholder.

'Twopence? It was only a penny last week.'

'Yeh, but the bread's twice as thick this week.'

'But what about the coffee? I didn't get twice as
much.'

'Nah, but it was twice as hot.'

Muttering under his breath about greedy stallholders who would steal the food out of the mouth
of a starving baby given half the chance, Pa bent
down to pick up his baskets.

It was a source of great pride to the porters of
Covent Garden that they could carry heavy loads
on their head. And even though their knees were
buckling under the weight of two or three baskets
full of vegetables and fruit, they all staggered along,
their teeth clenched, their shirts wet with sweat –
all, that is, except Pa Perkinski. Picking up four
baskets, each filled to the brim with potatoes and
onions, he balanced them on the woven knot all

porters wore on their head and walked away as if they were no heavier than a bowler hat.

Pa was well known in the market for he had worked there in the busy summer season for as long as he could remember. Even so, there were many newcomers up from the country, men in smocks and old straw hats, their wives in plain skirts and old-fashioned bonnets, who gawped in amazement at Pa as he strolled by.

Since he was well over six feet tall and his baskets towered above him, anybody perched on the top of Pa's load – an unlikely occurrence – would have had a fine view of the vast square that stretched from Long Acre to the Strand on one side and from Bow Street to Bedford Street on the other.

Hundreds of stalls piled high with vegetables, fruit and flowers were engulfed by a great sea of people – housewives pausing to examine bunches of glossy white leeks, costermongers in their corduroy waistcoats and flared trousers haggling over crates of purple-tinged broccoli, greengrocers from London's suburbs frowning and counting their money, beggars pleading, 'Give a copper to a poor fellow as hasn't eaten for months, guv' – and every-where boys, boys of every age, shape and size, following their coster fathers around the market to learn the trade, selling second-hand and frequently rotten produce thrown away by stallholders, running errands, carrying messages and generally being a help or a hindrance, depending on their wont.

'Cut away there, guv! Shove on one side, missus!' Pa shouted as he elbowed his way through the crowd. But even his strong voice was lost in the horrendous din of thousands of traders all bellowing their wares until they were hoarse – 'Twopence a pound, pears. Ho ho ho!' 'Handful of parsley a penny. Hi hi hi!' 'Pineapples, ha'penny a slice. Come and look!' 'Penny a lot, fine russets. Buy buy buy!'

A woman with two purple pickling cabbages under one arm and a cauliflower as big as a football under the other fell heavily on the flagstones, which were slimy with fallen leaves. The cabbages rolled one way and the cauliflower the other. Immediately small, grimy hands reached out to grab them.

'Thieves!' the woman shrieked. 'Stop them. Thieves!'

But by the time she was back on her feet her morning's shopping was well on its way to the other side of the market, there to be sold at a handsome profit.

Pa yawned, revealing a fine set of gums with one or two teeth placed at strategic intervals. He'd been up since four and there was still a while to go before the market closed at midday. For hours he'd carried baskets of turnips and cucumbers and celery from shops and stalls to the costermongers' pony and donkey barrows and handcarts that filled every street around Covent Garden for as far as the eye could see.

He was loading his baskets into one of these when he heard someone shout, 'Bert! Bert!' and he turned to see a costermonger charging up the street, his hobnailed boots practically striking sparks off the cobblestones in his haste.

'What's up, Arthur?' said Pa.

'Got a bit of bad news,' said his brother. 'I've just heard that Killer Kelly's out of prison.'

'What, already? I thought he got two years for hammerin' them navvies.'

'He did. But he's done his time. And you'd best keep out of his way, Bert.'

'Why? Just cos I helped myself to the money he owed me? Nah, he'll have forgotten all about it.'

'Forgotten? Killer Kelly? You must be off your chump.' Uncle Arthur shook his head in disbelief at Pa's naivety. 'Killer Kelly never forgets nothin'. Remember what he did to Mick Mullins and Jed Clark and—?'

'Yeh, yeh, I know he's an ugly customer, but don't you worry, Arthur, I can handle him. What's he doin' now, d'you know? Is he back at the Fancy?'

'Yeh, he's takin' on all-comers in a field up in King's Cross. That's provided the crushers don't tumble to it.'

Pa shook his head. 'They won't go nowhere near. They know they'd get a right pastin' if they did. When's the fight start?'

'Couple of hours. Slippery Sid's up first.'

'Old Slip? He won't last one round against Killer Kelly,' scoffed Pa. 'The only bloke that can beat him is me.'

A look of consternation passed over his brother's face. 'You're not goin' to take him on, are you, Bert?' he said nervously.

'Course I am. I got three more loads to shift and I'll be on my way.'

'Don't do it!' Uncle Arthur put a hand on his brother's hand. 'You'll regret it. Bert, listen to me.'

'I got to do it, Arthur.' Pa pushed his hand away. 'I haven't had a fight in months, not a good one, and I need the ready real bad.'

5

With many a cuff and blow to urge them on, Jem
and Ned were hurried through a maze of narrow
streets in Seven Dials, past shabby houses with
broken windows filled with brown paper and doors
falling from their hinges or ripped off for firewood.
Women in rags sat on the pavement chatting while
their children, who were almost naked, scavenged
alongside rats and mangy cats for scraps to eat in
the huge piles of filth and rubbish that stood at
every street corner.

'Right, here we are,' said Captain, stopping in
front of a narrow three-storey house. 'Go on up,
Goose,' he said to a boy with a mouth that seemed
to stretch from one ear to the other.

Still struggling and protesting their innocence,
Jem and Ned were hauled up a steep staircase and
thrust into a small room with a ceiling so low that
some of the taller children could barely stand
upright. A large bed covered in dirty blankets was

the only furniture in the room and the floor was covered in straw.

'You three, stand at the back against the wall,' Captain instructed Jem, Ned and Billy. 'And the rest of you, stop shovin'!' he complained as a dozen or more children piled into the room, all jostling for space. 'Right, court's in session. Bring forward the prisoners, Goose.'

'I can't, Captain,' said Goose, trying to push his way through the crowd. 'I can't move.'

'All right, the prisoners'll have to stay where they are. What's your names?'

'Jem Perkinski and—'

'Perkinski?' Captain frowned. 'That's not a proper name.'

'It is!'

'Nah, it must be Perkins.'

'It's Perkinski, I'm tellin' you,' insisted Jem. 'We come from a famous gypsy family . . . We do!' he cried indignantly as the other children burst out laughing.

'Paff! You're never no gypsies,' jeered a feisty girl with a mass of bright red ringlets that jounced and jingled every time she moved her head. 'Ralph's a gypsy, a proper one.' She pointed at a boy with dark hair and a swarthy complexion.

'Yeh, that's right, Ruby, we're Romanies,' he said proudly.

'Ah, well, we're . . . er . . . we're Rookeries,' said Jem. 'We're better than you lot.'

'I've never heard of no gypsies called Rook—'

'Yeh, yeh, all right, let's get on with it,' interrupted Captain. 'What're the names of them two?'

'This is my brother Ned and the little one's Billy. I'm the oldest.'

'But I'm the biggest,' said Ned.

'You're not,' retorted Jem. 'It's just that your hair sticks up.'

'Nah, it doesn't. I'm at least an inch taller than—'

'Stash it, the pair of you,' snapped Captain. 'Goose, tell them the verdict of the court.'

'Oy, we want to know what we're charged with first,' said Jem, for he and Ned had appeared before the magistrates before and knew what went on in a court of law.

Captain sighed. 'Go on, Goose, read it out.'

'Er . . . right,' said the boy. And he produced a very scruffy piece of paper on which were written two nursery rhymes and a rude joke. But neither he nor any of the other children knew that because none of them could read. 'The charge is that them three nicked Clara Forbes's broom and bagged her crossin' and didn't give her nothin'.'

'That's cos we didn't make nothin',' said Jem.

'That don't matter,' retorted Captain. 'You got to pay a fine of ten shillin's and if you can't pay it –' he clenched his fists in anticipation – 'you'll get a right walloper.'

6

Well before midday an eerie silence had fallen over Covent Garden. Shopkeepers who usually stayed open until they'd sold their last shallot closed and bolted their doors and put up the shutters. Traders in the market grasped the handles of their stalls and wheeled them away. As for the costermongers, a few were still roaming the streets trying to sell their produce, but most were already on their way to the fight.

'Where's everyone gone?' demanded an irate housewife, arriving late with an empty basket on her arm. 'I got to buy a bit of beef and some taters and greens. My old man'll kill me if I don't get somethin' for his dinner tomorrow.'

'They're all at the Fancy,' said one of the small boys who worked in the market by day and slept among the baskets at night. 'Bert the Beast's fightin' Killer Kelly up in King's Cross. Some toff's backin' Kelly. They say he's put up a purse of sixty guineas.

But our lot's matched it,' he added proudly, 'cos we know Bert'll win.'

'When's the fight start?'

'Within the hour, I reckon.'

'King's Cross,' muttered the woman. 'If I was to run all the way, I might be in time.' And she set off, skirts flying.

'Taters, twopence a bag!' shouted a girl who'd been left to sell the last of the vegetables on her father's stall. 'Tell you what, missus, I'll make it a penny a bag and throw in a pound of fresh greens. That'll make a nice Sunday dinner for you and the kids.'

'Nah.' The woman rushed past, shaking her head. 'I'm not wastin' the ready on vittals. I'm puttin' it on Bert the Beast.'

Pa was right when he said the police would go nowhere near a bare-knuckle fight. For most of the first half of the century prize-fighting had been the underworld's favourite sport and the police could not impose a code of decent conduct on the boxers or their followers since the Fancy was illegal.

This had never stopped gentlemen from the upper classes turning up in their smart carriages or astride horses to watch their favourites thrash each other, and the old Prince Regent himself had often been seen at the ringside, surrounded by his courtiers. But those days had long gone. A shameful contest in 1845 between the reigning champion, Ben Caunt, and a blackguard nicknamed Bendigo had finally dragged the sport into the gutter. And there it stayed, supported by the lowest of the low – and Pa – which was why the police rarely appeared, for they knew they had little chance of imposing the law on a mob so vicious they would have thought nothing of slicing policemen into bite-size pieces and feeding them to their dogs.

News of the fight between Pa and Killer Kelly spread through London like wildfire and hundreds of people, including many of Pa's relatives, hurried to the field in King's Cross.

Standing in the back of Uncle Arthur's donkey cart, acknowledging the deafening cheers of his followers with a confident smile and wave, Pa arrived in time to see Slippery Sid carted off to the nearest hospital for what would be, from the look of him, a very long stay.

'Shove over!' shouted Uncle Arthur, trying to get to the ring. 'Make way for the champion.'

'Champion?' jeered one of Killer Kelly's fans. 'He looks more like a chump to me.'

'And your bloke looks more like a baboon to me,' Uncle Arthur sniggered. 'Where did his mum and dad live – in them zoology gardens in Regent's Park?'

'Here, you shut your kisser, cabbage-head, or I'll shut it for you,' snarled the man. And he lashed out at Uncle Arthur.

Immediately there was a scuffle and before Pa had got within fifty yards of the ring a fight had broken out between the opposing factions. As both sides had come well armed with a variety of lethal weapons, from coshes to shovels, they set about each other with all the ferocity of gladiators.

A man soberly dressed in a stovepipe hat and black suit pushed his way to the front of the howling mob and, taking a sheet of paper from his pocket, he began to declaim in a loud voice, 'There are some misguided individuals in this country who oppose the noble art of fist fighting. But I contend that it is a strong force for moral good. It encourages the manly virtues. It promotes justice and that sense of fair play for which the British are justly famed. It preserves . . .' But nobody heard what fist fighting preserved because the man was clobbered before he could finish.

Pa got out of the cart and, landing the occasional

punch on someone's nose to persuade them to get out of his way, he finally arrived at the ring, where Killer Kelly was leaning against the ropes waiting for him.

Killer Kelly was one of the best bare-knuckle fighters in the country and by far the most brutal. He had thrashed many a man to within an inch of his life and left many more dead or dying from their injuries. Tall and lithe, with a hard, compact body, he was quick on his feet and could weave and feint until his opponent was confused and giddy. Behind his scarred and misshapen face with its bulbous eyes and lantern jaw lurked a shrewd brain, but he was cursed with a foul temper and, if crossed, a thirst for revenge that invariably led him into trouble, which was why he had spent most of his life breaking rocks in Pentonville at Her Majesty's pleasure or treading the mill in the Steel.

On the rare occasions he was out of prison, his prowess had earned him the patronage of Lord Hurdon, the son of an ancient and noble family, whose manners and morals were more appropriate to a pigsty than a mansion in Berkshire. But he had money and plenty of it. And it was his dubious pleasure to follow Killer Kelly around the country putting up the purse for his fights.

He sat now in his carriage on the outskirts of the vast crowd, from which vantage point he could see all that was happening – Pa and Killer Kelly both stripped to the waist glaring at each other, their supporters trading insults and blows. Though the fight had not yet begun, the scene was already one of utter chaos. And from the expression on Lord Hurdon's face, he was clearly enjoying it.

'This is great sport,' he said, laughing heartily as yet another man fell to the ground, his nose or ribs broken, his face bruised and torn.

7

At the crossing sweepers' court the children pressed forward, eager to see Captain punish Jem, Ned and Billy, for he was a big fellow, well capable of inflicting nasty cuts and bruises in painful places.

'You got to find us guilty first,' protested Jem.

'Well, we do.'

'You got to prove it. You got to bring in witnesses and stuff.'

Captain heaved a sigh. 'This is a waste of time,' he complained. 'We know you're guilty cos we all saw you do it.'

'But we got to do it proper, Captain,' said Goose, 'like when one of us is brought up before the beak.'

'Oh, all right, bring in the first witness.'

'It's Clara Forbes, only she isn't here.'

'Yeh, I am,' cried a small voice. 'I'm at the bottom of the stairs.'

'Shove to one side, you lot!' shouted Captain. 'Let her up, Lor's sake!'

After a great deal of pushing and elbowing, the girl with the button eyes finally appeared.

'Swear her, Goose,' said Captain.

'All right. Clara Forbes, raise your right hand and say after me—'

'There ought to be a Bible,' protested Jem. 'She's got to swear on the Bible.'

Goose frowned. 'Anyone got a Bible?'

'I got a book called *The Romin' Conquest of Brixton*,' said a boy at the back of the room. 'I nicked it off a spiffy old codger. He was sittin' in the park readin' it.'

'How d'you know what it's called?' said Captain.

'Cos he told me.'

'What, after you'd nicked it?'

'Course not, don't be daft. I sat next to him and asked him civil like what he was readin' and he said he was uncommon pleased that a toerag the likes of me should be interested in books and he gave it me.'

'I thought you said you nicked it.'

'I did. He gave it me to look at the pictures and I ran off quick as old boots. I reckon I'll get a tanner for it from a swag-shop.'

'That'll do. Pass it over,' said Goose impatiently. 'Now, Clara, put your paw on it and say after me—'

'I know, I know, I've done it before,' said the girl. 'I swear to tell the truth, whole truth'n nothin' like, s'help me God,' she proclaimed in a loud voice.

'Right, tell us what happened,' said Goose.

'Nah, wait a minute,' protested Jem. 'We don't know who she is.'

'What d'you mean, we don't know? She's Clara. We've known her since she was—'

'She's got to give us her name and age and address like in a proper court of law,' insisted Jem.

'Oh blimey!' Goose exclaimed impatiently. 'Oh, go on then, Clara, tell him.'

'My name's Clara Forbes and I'm seven years old, I think, and my address is . . .' She frowned, giving it some thought. Then she shrugged and said, 'Anywhere.'

'That'll do,' said Goose, glaring at Jem, defying him to hold up the proceedings of the court any longer. 'Get on with it.'

The children listened attentively as Clara told the court what had happened in Trafalgar Square that morning.

'You mean *that* boy –' Captain pointed at Jem – 'told you your brother'd been run over by a omnibus and you didn't *suspect nothin*?' he said, shaking his head in amazement.

'Yeh,' said Clara.

'And you let him have your broom cos he promised he'd give you half what he took – and you *believed him?*'

'Yeh,' said Clara, bristling at the implied criticism in his voice. 'You would've too,' she added hotly. 'He's the best liar I ever come across.'

There were murmurs of admiration from the other crossing sweepers.

'He's a real pro,' said one.

'Yeh, he's a sharp bloke and no kiddin',' said another.

'But him and his brothers are still thieves, even though they're the best we ever met,' insisted Captain, as Jem, Ned and Billy swelled with pride.

'Yeh, Captain's right,' agreed the other children. 'They're guilty as charged. They should be punished.'

'Come on then,' said Captain, holding up his fists, 'Give us ten shillin's or . . .'

'Oh Lor',' muttered Ned. 'Now we're in for it.'

'Is he goin' to paste us?' whispered Billy, hiding behind his brothers.

'Course not,' said Jem confidently.

'Oh? And why not?' snapped Captain, who was itching to land a punch on Jem's nose.

'Cos we got the ready.'

'Paff!' sneered Captain. 'You've never got ten shillin's.'

'Nah, we haven't,' agreed Billy.

'But our pa has. And if you go to Devil's Acre,' said Jem, winking at Ned, 'he'll give it you.'

'As well as one in the breadbasket,' grinned Ned.

'Oh yeh? I'd like to see the old fogey as can drop me one,' Captain crowed. ''Less, of course, it just so happens your pa's a prize fighter,' he added, doubling up with laughter at the very idea.

'Matter of fact, he is,' said Jem.

'*What?*'

'A prize fighter . . . their pa's a prize fighter,' the other children whispered to each other, looking at the Perkinski brothers with awe, for a bare-knuckle boxer was a hero in their eyes.

'He's a champion, name of Bert the Beast,' said Jem. 'You probably heard of him. He gen'rally fights at the Queen's Head, off Windmill Street. He beat Jack "The Giant Killer" Jackson there.'

'And Jed the Jabber,' said Ned.

'And Duck-feet Doug,' said Billy.

'Our pa's got a nasty temper, hasn't he, Ned?'

'Uncommon nasty, Jem. 'Specially when someone asks him for the ready. Sends him ravin' looney, that does.'

'Remember that bloke that said Pa owed him ten shillin's?' Jem said, watching Captain's reaction out of the corner of his eye. 'Pa broke every bone in his body.'

'And ripped off his skin.'

'And pulled out his hair.'

'And his teeth.'

'And chucked him in the river.'

'Nah, he didn't,' piped up Billy. 'Pa gave him a shillin' and said he'd pay him the rest, a tanner a week.'

'Stall your mug,' growled Jem, giving him a pinch on the bottom to shut him up.

Captain stepped back, nonplussed. Though he was a strong boy and courageous when necessary, he knew it would be foolhardy to take on a bare-knuckle fighter, especially one with the fearsome reputation of Bert the Beast.

'Ah . . . well . . . uhm . . . there seems to have been a bit of a misunderstandin' here. If you'd only let me finish,' he said, looking aggrieved, 'I was goin' to say that we'd let you off – that's assumin' you were guilty as charged, which, of course, you're not,' he added quickly. 'Anyway, I was goin' to say we'd let you off if you were members of the TSADCSA, cos members are allowed to borrow each other's brooms and stuff.'

'What's the TD . . . TC . . . what you just said?' Jem frowned.

'The Trafalgar Square and District Crossin' Sweepers' Association.'

'Never heard of it.'

'Well, you have now.'

'But what if we don't want to be members of the TC . . . TS . . . the what you said?' said Jem.

'You barmy or somethin'?' exclaimed Captain. 'Every kid in London wants to be one of us.'

'They're fightin' to get in,' said Goose.

'Why? There's no money in sweepin' crossin's.'

'Not now cos it's hot and the streets are dry but when it starts rainin' and snowin' you can make a killin'.'

'I reckon we should have a go, Jem. Gran says it's goin' to rain tomorrow,' said Ned.

'Course it isn't, you stupe.'

'Gran says her bunions are hurtin' somethin' awful and that means it's goin' to be wet. Besides, I want to do it.' Ned jutted out his chin. 'It's an honest livin'. Well,' he faltered, unnerved by the

44

hush that had descended on the noisy room, 'it is, isn't it?'

Jem stared at his feet, red-faced with embarrassment, while Goose cupped a hand to his ear, a puzzled expression on his face, as if he couldn't quite believe what he'd heard. Someone tittered and the titter became a chuckle and the chuckle became a giggle and the giggle became a guffaw and then all the children were roaring with laughter, clutching their sides as tears flowed down their cheeks.

Above it all Jem could be heard shouting, 'Ned didn't mean it. He was only kiddin'. He was! He was!'

8

According to the London Prize Rules there had to be two umpires at a bare-knuckle fight, one chosen by each side, and an impartial referee chosen by common agreement.

Pa nominated Uncle Arthur as his umpire and Killer Kelly opted for his manager, Tom Darling, an inaptly named man with a face like a hyena and an attitude to match.

Finding a referee who would favour neither side was more of a problem, however. Pa put forward Jim Turner, proclaiming that he had never clapped eyes on him before. This produced an immediate outcry from Killer Kelly's camp. 'That's Bert's cousin, lives in Lambeth, works at a butcher's,' shouted one man. 'He's a right screw too,' he added bitterly. 'He's always givin' my missus short weight.'

There followed a flurry of blows between the two men and Cousin Jim was declared unacceptable as a referee. Killer Kelly then proposed someone who turned out to be his father. 'But I haven't seen him since before I was born,' he protested as the old man was laughed out of the ring. 'How was I to know he's my dad?'

One by one both men's fathers, brothers, brothers-in-law, nephews, uncles, cousins, friends and fans were eliminated until it began to look as if there was nobody who qualified as an unbiased referee.

'What about him?' suggested Lord Hurdon, pointing with his cane at a tramp curled at the foot of a tree, fast asleep. Immediately the poor old man was seized by three or four ruffians. Protesting loudly, 'I haven't done nothin'. I'm a good bloke, a decent bloke, I never pinched nothin' from no one,' he was frogmarched into the ring, which was no more than a rope suspended between four poles in the middle of a field.

After the reason for his being there was explained to him the tramp whined, 'But I don't know nothin' about fightin'. I never been to a fight in my life.'

'That doesn't matter,' said Uncle Arthur. 'The thing is —' he pointed at his brother and Killer Kelly — 'd'you know them two blokes?'

Now if the tramp had been smarter he would

have said yes, he knew them as well as the back of his hand, if not better, but thirty years of shuffling along the open road in all weathers, sleeping in derelict barns or ditches and eating what little he could beg or steal, had dulled his brain. He squinted at the two fighters with rheumy eyes and shook his head.

'You never seen them before?' said Uncle Arthur.

'Nah.'

'You sure?' said Tom Darling.

'I'm tellin' you, I don't know them; I never seen them before and I don't like the look of them neither. Can I go now?'

The two umpires looked at each other and for the first and last time that day found themselves in agreement.

'Right.' They nodded. 'He'll do.'

'Will I get paid for it?' asked the tramp hopefully.

'Oh yeh, you'll get paid all right. You'll get paid with this,' threatened Tom Darling, thrusting his fist under the tramp's nose, 'if you don't do it fair and square.'

'Right,' said Uncle Arthur, 'You ready, Bert?'

Pa nodded.

'You ready, Kelly?' asked his umpire.

Killer Kelly nodded.

'Referee, start the fight.'

'I don't know what to do,' whined the tramp.

'You got to tell them to come up to the scratch,' explained Uncle Arthur, pointing to a line painted across the middle of the ring.

'Oh . . . oh right . . . uhm . . . gen'lemen, come up to the scratch.'

Pa and Killer Kelly stepped forward until their toes were touching the line and their noses were pressed flat against each other.

'I been wantin' to meet you again,' growled Killer Kelly. 'All the time I was in prison I kept thinkin' I must find Bert when I get out so's he can give me back the money he pinched from my pocket when I was too drunk to stop him.'

'I won that money, Kelly, but you wouldn't give it me,' protested Pa.

'You never won it, Bert.'

'You wagered me five guineas I couldn't carry eight baskets on my head from one side of the market to the other.'

'And you didn't.'

'I did.'

'But them baskets were all empty.'

'That's right.'

'Paff! Any measly cove can carry eight *empty*

baskets. Even my grandmother could carry eight *empty* baskets.'

'You didn't say they'd got to be full.'

'You know damned fine I meant—'

'Get on with it,' Jim Darling hissed in the tramp's ear, 'or they'll have killed each other before the fight starts.'

'What've I got to do?' muttered the tramp, backing away from the irate pugilists.

'Tell them to start, of course, you numbskull.'

But it was too late, for the two boxers had already set about each other.

'Go and stand outside the ring,' Uncle Arthur said to the tramp, pushing him out of harm's way. 'It's up to me and Tom Darlin' to see the fight's clean,' he explained, as Pa forced Killer Kelly's arm up his back and did his best to wrench it off, 'but if we don't agree about somethin', you got to make the final decision. So you got to watch carefully all the time. Do you tumble to what I'm sayin'? I said, d'you understand?' shouted Uncle Arthur, trying to make himself heard above the bellowing of the crowd.

'Yeh.' The tramp nodded. And he ducked under

the rope, crouched down, squeezed his eyes tightly shut and buried his head in his knees.

If he had watched he would have seen that the two boxers had very distinctive styles. Pa was twice as wide and at least five stone heavier than his opponent, with a huge barrel of a chest and muscles a carthorse would have been proud of. Clasping Killer Kelly above the waist he used his great weight to wrestle him to the ground in the hope of crushing the life out of him. But the other boxer used his wits as well as his fists and just when Pa thought he had him to rights he skittered away, leaving Pa floundering.

Killer Kelly's technique was more sophisticated. As light and agile on his feet as Pa was heavy and lumbering, time and again he attacked ferociously but dropped down on one knee with a hand to the ground before Pa could retaliate. Since it was a foul to hit a man when he was down – and Killer Kelly always put on a great show of being badly hurt – Pa had to wait for him to get up before the fight could continue. Killer Kelly would stay down for a second or two, then, choosing his moment, spring up, catching Pa off guard and giving him a vicious blow before dancing away again.

And so it continued for round after round, Pa

trying in vain to force the other man to the ground, Killer Kelly dropping to one knee before Pa could land a blow with his massive fists.

'Foul! Foul! Foul!' yelled Pa's supporters. 'Killer Kelly's cheatin' like a brick!'

'Nah, it's Bert the Beast who's fightin' dirty,' retorted Killer Kelly's followers – and in no time at all the two factions were going at each other with a vengeance.

The tramp opened one eye, saw the mayhem raging around him and crawled back into the ring for safety. But there was no safe place, nowhere to hide from the howling mob, and even Killer Kelly was knocked out briefly by a flying cudgel.

'One of your lot did that,' protested Tom Darling, throwing a bucket of water over Killer Kelly's head to bring him round.

'Nah, it wasn't,' retorted Uncle Arthur. 'It was one of your lot.'

'Why would one of our lot knock out their own man?' scoffed Tom Darling.

'Cos they're a load of half-baked, addlepated fat-heads – and that includes you.'

Not surprisingly this impolite exchange between the umpires resulted in their engaging each other in a punch-up, so that by the end of the ninety-fifth round there were two sets of boxers in the ring. And since Uncle Arthur and Tom Darling were going at it hammer and tongs, theirs appeared to be the far more interesting contest.

The mood of the crowd turned even uglier. Frustrated that neither prize fighter seemed to be gaining the ascendancy, each faction turned against their own man.

'Get up, you crawler!' they yelled at Killer Kelly as he dropped to his knees for the umpteenth time. 'You're supposed to be fightin', not prayin'.'

'Havin' a nice nap, Bert?' they hollered as Pa, finding himself punching thin air, threw himself to the ground yet again. 'Chuck him a pillow, someone, he's feelin' a bit crawly mawly.'

Incensed that anyone would accuse him of being a weakling, Pa heaved himself upright and, clenching his fist, he took a swing at Killer Kelly that should have knocked him into the next world. But Killer Kelly ducked and the blow caught Uncle Arthur smack on the jaw. He staggered back, a look of puzzlement on his face, before keeling over.

The crowd erupted into hoots of derisive laughter as he was dragged from the ring.

'You got to choose another umpire, Bert,' said Tom Darling.

'Right,' said Pa, 'I'll have my cousin Jim.'

'Nah, you won't. I'm not havin' that swindlin' butcher in this ring.'

'Percy'll do it then.'

'Don't shake hands with him, Tom,' someone in the crowd warned him as Pa's youngest brother clambered into the ring. 'He's a pure finder.'

'And he's brought some of it with him, by the smell of him,' shouted another, for there was certainly a strong whiff of dog droppings about Uncle Percy.

At that everyone in the front few rows slapped a hand over their nose and gasped, 'Phew!'

9

'You goin' to join us or not?' demanded Captain.

'Yeh,' Jem nodded, 'and let's get on with it. Me and Ned and Billy should be out earnin' the ready—'

'Hold hard, we got to do the secret ceremony first. Goose, go and get Mother Bailey's knife from the kitchen, the real sharp one she uses for cuttin' up bones.'

'What d'you want that for?' said Ned, gulping hard.

'To get some of your blood, of course. We can't have a secret ceremony without blood.'

'Nah. Nah, you're not takin' none of mine. I need it. All of it.'

'It's only a couple of drops, you lily-livered ninny,' scoffed Ruby.

'Come on, stick out your right hand,' Captain said to the three brothers when Goose returned with a very evil-looking butcher's knife. 'I'm goin' to cut your finger. Just a bit,' he added comfortingly as Ned made a bolt for the door, followed by Billy. But Jem thrust out his little finger and said, 'Well, go on. Get on with it.'

Captain inserted the tip of the blade into Jem's finger and a tiny trickle of blood threaded its way down his palm.

'Is he dead yet?' whispered Billy.

'Not yet,' said Ned.

'We all rub your blood on us,' Captain explained to Jem as the crossing sweepers lined up, 'cos that makes us brothers—'

'And sisters,' cut in Ruby.

'I was just goin' to say that,' retorted Captain. 'We swear to watch out for each other and protect each other—'

'To the death.'

'Will you shut up, Ruby! I'm doin' this.'

'Get on with it then.'

'Go on, Goose, you start,' said Captain.

The boy stepped forward and placing his little finger over Jem's he said in a solemn voice, 'Your friends are my friends, your enemies are my enemies. So be it. All right, Ethel, your turn,' he said to a pretty, dark-skinned girl.

'Your friends are my friends, your enemies are

my enemies. So be it,' she intoned. And then, before Jem could duck, she gave him a kiss on the cheek.

'Oy!' he exclaimed, scrubbing his face furiously. 'Why'd she do that?'

'Reckon she's spoony on you,' sniggered Captain. 'All right, Ruby, stop pushin', you're next.'

'He hasn't go no blood left,' complained the girl, peering at Jem's finger. 'Give him another jab, Captain,' she said eagerly.

'Nah,' protested Jem. 'Why me? Why don't you jab *her* finger?'

'Cos it's got to be your blood,' said Captain, picking up the knife.

'It's all right, it's all right, I got some more,' said Jem quickly, giving his finger a good squeeze. 'Look, there's loads of it. I reckon I got enough for half of London.'

Quickly the other crossing sweepers swore the oath.

'Good.' Captain nodded approvingly. 'Now *they've* got to do it,' he said, pointing at Ned and Billy, who were cowering in a corner.

'Nah, you got enough blood from me for the three of us,' said Jem. 'Besides, Billy's so small he hasn't got none.'

'Oh, all right,' said Captain, putting the knife

 57

down reluctantly. 'So now it's official. Jem, Ned and Billy Parsonski —'

'Perkinski.'

'You lot are members of the TSADCSA. Goose, read them the rules.'

'Rule Number One,' said Goose, producing the same scruffy piece of paper as before and pretending to read. 'If you see two gen'lemen about to cross the road you sing out, "Two toffs!" and they're yours. But if I was to see them first, they'd be mine. If we both see them at the same time, we share the money — that's always provided they give us some,' he added with a grimace. 'If you see a gen'leman and a lady, you shout, "A toff and a doll!" and if the gent has a lady on each arm, you shout, "A sandwich". But if I see them first and you cut me up, I'll give you a good hidin'.'

'What's Rule Number Two?' asked Ned.

'There isn't one,' said Goose, putting the piece of paper back in his pocket.

'All right, everyone, back to work,' shouted Captain. 'Billy, you go with Betty and see if you can get us some grub for supper,' he said, indicating a girl even smaller than Billy. 'She'll show you what to do. And you two can share the crossin' with Clara,' he said to Jem and Ned.

'Why've I got to share my crossin' with them?' demanded Clara.

'It's just for today, so's they can learn the ropes. We'll find another pitch for them tomorrow.'

10

By the hundred and twentieth round both boxers were beginning to weaken. They had been in the ring for more than three hours and it looked as if they'd still be there at midnight, since neither was winning . . . And then Pa changed his tactics.

After a series of lethal jabs at Pa's ribcage Killer Kelly went in for the kill, but for once it was Pa who feigned injury and dropped to his knee with one hand on the floor. Killer Kelly was momentarily confused at having the tables turned on him but before he could slide away Pa began to get up and dealt him a punishing blow.

Clutching his belly Killer Kelly slumped forward, groaning.

'Get up!' Tom Darling hissed at him. 'You got to come up to the scratch or you're out of the fight.'

'I can't,' the stricken boxer gasped. 'He's punched a bloody great hole in my tripes.'

'Foul! Foul!' screamed his supporters.

Not surprisingly, the two umpires failed to agree, Tom Darling insisting that Pa's blow was well below the belt, Uncle Percy protesting it was Killer Kelly's fault for wearing his belt so high.

They appealed to the referee.

'Come on, wake up,' snapped Tom Darling, giving him an encouraging kick.

'What d'you want?' The tramp peered at him through his fingers.

'You got to say Killer Kelly won the fight cos Bert the Beast cheated.'

'He did not,' exclaimed Uncle Percy. 'Bert played fair and square. It's your man who's been fightin' dirty all through.'

'Well?' The two umpires glared at the tramp.

'Well what?' he said.

'WHICH ONE'S THE WINNER?'

The tramp began to tremble violently. 'How do I know?' he cried.

'COS YOU'RE THE REFEREE.'

The tramp looked at Killer Kelly, who was still writhing on the ground moaning about his 'tripes', and then at Pa Perkinski, who towered over him, his huge body glistening with blood and sweat, his biceps standing up like steel-hard hillocks.

'Him,' he whispered, pointing at Pa with a trembling hand.

At that all hell broke loose. Pa's fans yelled in triumph while Killer Kelly's bellowed with disgust.

'The referee was bribed!' they raged. 'The fight was fixed!'

At the height of the uproar a large contingent of London's constabulary arrived. Provoked beyond measure by the enormity of the crowd and the violence of their behaviour, they charged on to the field and springing their rattles and wielding their wooden truncheons set to with considerable zest. Within minutes many of the spectators were sprawled on the ground and many more were being hustled into police carts.

'We'd best get out of here plaguy quick, Bert,' said Uncle Percy, 'or they'll cop us too.'

'Nah, I'm not goin' till I get my prize money,' said Pa.

Tom Darling sniggered. 'You can go whistle for it.'

'But I won it. It's mine by rights. I won it fair'n square.'

'Fair'n square?' barked Killer Kelly, struggling painfully to his feet, his face contorted in fury. 'You cheated me out of this fight like you cheated me out of my money – Oh yeh, you did,' he snarled, waving aside Pa's protests. 'But I'll get you for it, see if I don't. Nobody cheats me and gets away with it.'

'Come on,' said Tom Darling urgently, grabbing his arm. 'Come on, Kelly. Them crushers'll nab us if we don't make a bolt for it and you'll be back in prison. Me too.'

'I'll get you, Bert!' Killer Kelly shouted over his shoulder as Tom Darling dragged him away. 'Don't matter where you hide, I'll find you. And when I do I'll . . .' He drew a finger across his throat. 'And good riddance.'

11

'This must be one of the best places to sweep crossin's, Clara,' said Jem as they followed the girl back to her pitch near the old church. 'I reckon the whole of London must walk by here.'

'Nah.' she shook her head. 'The quiet streets where the toffs live are best. There's a cove that works Cavendish Square. He's always outside the Duke of Portland's mansion. He makes near a shillin' a day. Last Christmas he took thirty-eight shillin's. And he gets good vittals from the cooks too, bits of beef and chicken left over from supper . . . Nah, don't even think about it,' she laughed as Jem's eyes lit up. 'He'd half kill you if you tried to take over his crossin'.'

'How much do you make, Clara?' asked Ned.

'In winter, when the streets are wet and muddy, about sixpence a day. But in good weather, like now –' she shrugged – 'I only make a farthin' or two, unless someone I know comes along. Some of the

ladies are kind to me. Just bow and lift your hat to them.'

But though Jem and Ned bowed and lifted their hats and took it in turns to sweep the road with the worn-out broom Captain had generously lent them till their backs ached and their arms were numb, no kind ladies came along and by nightfall they were tired and penniless.

'I'm right done up,' said Clara, yawning. 'Let's go back and see what Betty and your brother've got us to eat.'

'You live with the other kids then?' asked Ned.

'Nah, I live with my mum. And my little brother Pip, of course,' she added, giving Jem a wicked grin. 'But I always eat supper with the sweepers.'

'We're on to a good thing here, Ned,' Jem whispered in his brother's ear when they got to the crossing sweepers' lodging. 'Supper here, then supper at home. Reckon our bellies'll be full after that lot.'

Twenty or more children were packed into the kitchen of the small house, where an old woman in a torn frilly cap and heavily stained apron was stirring a steamy cauldron on the stove.

'Who's she?' asked Jem.

'Mother Bailey. And this is her paddin' ken,' said

Clara. 'She lets out rooms threepence a night. Them lot –' she pointed at the other children – 'all doss in the room upstairs cos they got nowhere else to go, apart from the gutter.'

'She goin' to make us pay for our vittals?' said Ned in alarm.

'Nah, we send the littlest kids out lookin' for stuff to eat and Mother Bailey cooks it for us. Very good to us, she is, provided we bring her things we find.'

'What kind of things?' asked Ned.

'Oh, things that've fallen out of people's pockets –' Clara winked at him impishly – 'like silk handkerchiefs and purses.'

'I've had enough of all this jawin',' complained Jem. 'I'm so hungry my belly thinks my throat's been cut.'

'There're only four bowls, so we got to wait our turn,' said Clara, elbowing smaller children out of the way.

'What's that?' frowned Ned, as the landlady ladled a thick, grey, pasty substance into a girl's bowl.

'Looks like the stuff they use to stick bricks together with,' said Jem. 'Go and ask Billy.'

Not surprisingly, Billy had been first in the

queue and was licking his bowl clean when Ned appeared.

'Lor',' said the little boy, beaming at his brother, 'that was golopshus.'

'Yeh? What was it?'

'Stuff me and Betty picked up from the gutter, like crusts of bread and apple cores and bones. Course, they were a bit dirty cos people'd trod on them, but Mother Bailey gave them a bit of a wash. She said nobody'd notice once she'd boiled them up.'

'What's up with you?' demanded Jem when Ned came back, his face as green as a frog's belly.

'I don't want no supper.'

'Crimes, neither do I,' muttered Jem once he knew what was in the steaming cauldron. 'Get Billy, we're goin'.'

12

Pa staggered into Devil's Acre, sloshed water over his face and body from an old rain barrel by the pigsty and shouted, 'Liza! Liza!'

'I'm here, Bert,' Ma called, opening the door of Gran's caravan and hurrying down the steps. 'I been helpin' the old girl make her magic potions all day. She's goin' to sell them at the fair next week and . . . Lawks a mercy,' she gasped when she saw Pa's battered and swollen face, 'you been run over by a omnibus, my pet?'

'Nah, I been in a fight.'

'And did you win?'

Pa started to nod, but his head hurt so much he changed his mind. 'Yeh,' he said.

Ma's eyes lit up. 'Jammy!' she cried. 'How much?'

'Nothin'. They wouldn't give me the purse cos they said I cheated. Which I didn't. I just gave Killer Kelly a dose of his own medicine.'

'Killer Kelly? Lor', Bert, you didn't take him on, did you? He's the most evil, cruel, black-hearted, vile brute this side of—'

'I know, I know, but I had to do it. We need the ready.'

'Not that much we don't,' retorted Ma hotly. 'I reckon you must be a stupe to fight a wicked bloke like—'

'Cheese it, Liza!' Pa snapped. 'We got no time to waste chatterin'. Killer Kelly's after me. He said he'd top me.'

'Oh, Bert!' Ma gasped. 'What're we goin' to do? What're we goin' to—'

'We'll go away for a bit. I know a nice, quiet yard back of Hungerford Market. Killer Kelly'll never find us there.'

'That's what you think,' said Ma, fear making her voice shake. 'He hounded Charlie White all over London and when he caught him he—'

'Hold your jaw!' roared Pa, who knew only too well what Killer Kelly and his thugs had done to the unfortunate man before dumping him in the Thames with a sack of bricks tied to his feet. 'Go and tell Gran we're off, while I put the chickens and pig in the caravan.'

'But we can't go yet, Bert. What about Jem, Ned and Billy?'

'I'll leave a message for them with Spud.'

'And Kate?'

'We'll stop at the Dog'n Bacon on the way out and pick her up. Lor's sake, woman, stir yourself!' Pa shouted, his nerves getting the better of him. 'Killer Kelly and his cronies'll be here any minute.'

13

'Where're we goin', Jem?' said Ned, trailing along behind him. 'We can't go home yet. We haven't made no money.'

'I know that, you goosecap. We're goin' up Drury Lane. The toffs'll be comin' out of the theatre about now, so we'll make a penny or two.'

But several hundred others had had the same idea.

Women weighed down by heavy trays were crying their wares – 'Twopence a pound, grapes! . . . Violets, lovely violets! . . . Ribbons, fine ribbons!' Stilt-dancers strutted above the crowd, occasionally crashing to the ground when someone barged into them. Sad old bears, tormented by the lash of their master's whip, lumbered from paw to paw in a parody of a dance. Jugglers balanced an umbrella on their nose while throwing balls, cups or knives in the air. Small boys did handstands and cartwheels. Small girls sang popular ballads – 'Mother, Is the

Battle Over?' and 'The Widow's Last Prayer' – in thin, mournful voices.

When the doors of the Theatre Royal opened there was a rush to surround the men in their top hats and satin-lined cloaks and women in evening dresses as they descended the steps.

'Buy! . . . Buy! . . . Give! . . . Give! . . . Spare a coin! . . . Please, guv! . . . Please, missus! Please!' begged the crowd as the theatre-goers hurried into the carriages and hansom cabs lined up at the kerb to whisk them away to restaurants and supper clubs in the more fashionable part of town.

'Let's go home,' said Jem, watching an agile boy curl himself into a tight ball and waddle along on his hands, begging everyone he passed to 'Give a poor little cripple a penny'.

'But Ma will—' began Ned.

'I know. Ma'll be snappish cos we haven't made no money, but we'll never get nothin' here.'

'Nah, I want somethin' to eat first,' said Billy, refusing to budge.

'You had supper.'

'Not proper supper. I want a hot potato. I want a bit of bread. I want—'

'We could go and see if we can get somethin' from the soup kitchen,' suggested Ned.

'Yeh, yeh, I want soup, want soup,' cried Billy, tugging at Jem's sleeve.

'You know we'll never get none. We never do,' complained Jem, who was being towed along the street by his very determined little brother. 'There'll be dozens of people there, hundreds, probably thousands. There, what did I tell you?' he said as they turned the corner into Drury Lane and saw the long, long line of hungry people waiting with their tin cans for the midnight soup kitchen to open. 'Millions of them! And we don't have nothin' to put the soup in anyway.'

'They could pour it straight in my mouth,' protested Billy.

'Well, I'm not standin' in line all night just to watch someone pour a drop of hot soup in your kisser,' snapped Jem. 'Come on, let's go. I said come on, Billy. Don't dawdle.'

It was a tired, hungry, dispirited trio that wound its way back through the dark streets to Devil's Acre. Jem and Ned trudged along in silence while Billy trailed way behind them, whining that he was 'dog-weary' and 'starvin'' and what he wanted most in all the world was a pork pie, even a tiny one – though he'd settle for a bowl of soup.

After a while his cries grew fainter and neither of

his brothers noticed when a coach came hurtling around the corner and the driver brought his team of horses to a halt with a curse.

'Look sharp there!' he shouted at the small figure curled up in the middle of the road. 'I nearly ran over you, you ninny. Cut away there, I say!' he stormed, as the horses tossed their heads and champed impatiently at their bits. 'Him with you, missus?' he asked a woman sitting in the gutter with a baby in her arms.

'Nah, he's with them, them down there.' She pointed at Jem and Ned, who were almost out of sight.

'Oy!' bellowed the coachman. 'Oy, you two! Come back here!'

The two boys came running back at the double.

'D'you know this kid?' said the coachman, pointing at Billy.

'That's our brother,' cried Jem, staring at Billy in horror. 'You've killed him.'

'Nah, he ain't dead,' said the coachman. 'Look.' He flicked Billy with his whip.

The little boy opened his eyes, muttered, 'G'night, Jem. G'night, Ned,' and went back to sleep.

'Get him off the road plaguy quick or I'll run over the lot of you,' growled the coachman. And he

whipped up his horses and sped away as Jem and Ned dragged Billy on to the pavement.

'Wake up!' Jem shook him hard. 'Lor's sake, Billy, stir your bones!'

'It's no use,' Ned said, 'he's out like a light. We'll have to carry him home between us. You take his legs and I'll—'

'Nah, let's doss down in one of them shop door-ways,' said Jem, secretly relieved at not having to face the wrath of his mother that night.

'But what if the crushers find us?' said Ned nervously.

'They won't, not if we curl up real small. Anyway, they won't see us in the dark.'

14

Clara walked quickly through the hot, crowded streets. She had no idea of the time, for only rich people had watches and clocks and Clara's family couldn't even afford a clock candle, but she knew it was after half past nine because all the shops were closing and the main thoroughfares of London were now full of revellers bent on enjoying themselves in theatres, restaurants and pubs.

Her walk quickened into a run. Her mother worked at night and she would be waiting for Clara to get back and look after the baby. But Clara had made no money that day and after her wretched supper at Mother Bailey's she had returned to her pitch in Trafalgar Square, sweeping horse manure and straw off the road in the hope that someone would give her a coin, if only a farthing. But in her drab, colourless rags nobody noticed her in the pale light of the gas lamps and all her efforts were in vain.

It was not the first time Clara had gone home empty-handed and though her mother never complained the girl felt ashamed. Abandoned by her husband shortly after the birth of her second child, Clara's mother had done her best to keep the small family together. But although Clara swept the streets all day and her mother worked through the night they were never more than one step away from poverty and the threat of the workhouse clung to them like a shroud.

That summer they were living in a dismal room on the top floor of a cheap lodging house which they shared with six or seven others, mostly tramps who spent a night or two sleeping on the bare boards before moving on. Her mother was standing in the doorway looking anxiously down the street when Clara ran up, panting. 'I'm . . . I'm sorry, Mum. I was tryin' to get some of the ready but—'

'Never mind that, my ducky,' said the woman. 'Go and see to Pip.'

'He still squally, Mum?'

'Yeh, and he's gettin' worse.'

'What's up with him?'

'I reckon he's got the molly grubs, though I'm sure I don't know why – the poor little mite's got next to nothin' in his belly.' And giving Clara a quick peck on the cheek her mother hurried away.

Wearily Clara climbed the steep stairs to the bleak room at the top of the house where the other inmates were sprawled across the floor, some in a deep sleep, others muttering and starting awake with a cry of alarm at some imagined danger.

Baby Pip was curled up in a pile of rags that passed for bedding, his face covered with flea bites which he scratched ineffectually with tiny fingers. He whimpered plaintively when he saw Clara and she wrapped her arms around him and rocked him gently, crooning soft words in his ear.

Soothed by the motion the baby began to quieten and, despite the snores and mutterings from the men and women around her and the overwhelming stench of pee and vomit, Clara too fell asleep, sitting bolt upright, her head lolling on her chest, but after an hour or two she was jolted awake by Pip's piercing screams.

'What's up, my tulip?' she said, kissing his cheek. The baby's skin was on fire and his whimpers turned to gasps, as if he was struggling to breathe.

'Oh no!' Clara recoiled in horror. 'Pip . . . Pip . . .'

'Shut up!' someone growled.

'But my brother – he's poorly. He—'

'Here, give him a swig of this —' the man held out a bottle of cheap gin. 'That'll keep him quiet . . . No?' He grinned as Clara shook her head. 'Have to drink it myself then.' And having emptied the remains of the gin down his throat he rolled over and began snoring thunderously.

The baby writhed in his sister's arms and thrashed his head feverishly from side to side.

Clara was frightened. 'Oh, Pip,' she murmured, her eyes filling with tears. 'Oh, Pip, I don't know what to do.'

There was no money for a doctor and Clara would never have taken him to a hospital, for they were perceived – and frequently with good reason – as places people went into alive and only came out of in a wooden box.

'Must find Mum,' she said, getting to her feet. 'Mum'll know what to do.'

Gingerly she stepped over the sleeping bodies to the door, trying not to step on an outstretched hand or foot, but the baby was heavy and she stumbled and almost fell.

'Hey, what you doin'?' demanded a woman, struggling upright. 'You stealin' from me? You tryin' to nick my—'

'Nah. Nah, I wasn't. I'm takin' my brother . . .

my mum . . . he's sick,' Clara stammered in confusion.

'What's wrong with him?' The woman's tone softened.

'I don't know. I got to get my mum. I got to—'

'Where is she, lovey?'

'She's workin'. In the Haymarket.'

'That's a long way to go with a littl'un. You'd best leave him here with me.'

Clara took a step back, hugging Pip protectively. The woman, like everyone else in the room, was a stranger to her, a beggar by the look of her torn, soiled clothes, who roamed the streets by day and slept in lodging houses by night if she'd been given a few coins – or in the gutter if she hadn't.

'You can't go traipsin' all over God's half-acre with a sick baby.' The woman reached out for Pip. 'Leave him here with me. He'll be all right.'

Again Clara hesitated. The woman was right; it was stupid to carry poor Pip all the way to the Haymarket on such a hot night and she would get there much faster without him. But . . . She gnawed her lip in an agony of indecision.

'Come on, give him to me. I know how to handle kids – I ought to by now, I've had nine,' the woman chuckled.

'All right.' Clara knelt down and put Pip in her arms. 'I'll be back—'

'Yeh, yeh, don't you worry, I'll still be here. Go on, off with you,' said the woman, waving her away. 'Go and get your mum.'

Clara ran like the wind, past the drunks staggering out of the pubs, their meagre funds squandered on gin and porter, past the burglars heading for the grand houses in Kensington and Belgravia, past the petty thieves on the lookout for careless people with silk kerchiefs dangling temptingly from their pockets.

Although she was only seven years old, Clara felt no fear. Unlike the children sleeping in their clean, dry beds in the respectable houses of London's suburbia, she was used to the corruption and depravity of the dark streets. A child of the slums, she knew of no other life and was unaware, or perhaps uncaring, of the dangers that lurked in every dark street and dingy courtyard.

Through the back lanes and alleyways she ran until she reached Coventry Street and turned down into Haymarket. Despite the lateness of the hour – or the earliness, since it was two o'clock in the morning – there were still crowds of people strolling along as if it was broad daylight.

'Please –' Clara ran up to a group of women who were chatting and laughing in loud, raucous voices. 'Please –' she tugged at a skirt to attract the wearer's attention – 'have you seen Flo Forbes?'

'Flo Forbes?' The woman squinted at her through eyelashes heavy with mascara. 'Never heard of her.'

'I know Flo,' said another woman. 'What d'you want with her?'

'My brother's poorly. I got to find her.'

'You Clara, are you?'

The girl nodded.

'Well, Clara, your mum's workin' at the moment.' She glanced over her shoulder at a dark alleyway.

'Then I'll go and—'

'Nah, you won't!' cried the woman, grabbing her. 'You go home like a good girl and as soon as your mum comes back I'll tell her. Go on, this is no place for you,' she said, giving Clara a gentle push.

'You will tell my mum.'

'Course I will, lovey. Soon as she gets back.'

Clara turned and ran. She was anxious to get back to Pip. Too late she had begun to doubt the wisdom of leaving him with a stranger. The woman had seemed kindly enough, but what if she had grown tired of the baby's whining and abandoned him? What if . . . ? Clara's heart lurched. What if she had stolen him? A beggar and a baby could wring far more money out of the soft-hearted than a beggar on her own, especially when the baby was as pretty as Pip.

'Please, oh please,' she muttered, 'let Pip be all right. Mum'll kill me if anything happens to him. Let Pip be – Oh!'

A cat streaked out of a doorway, tripping her up. She fell headlong, banging her chin and scraping strips of flesh from her knees and elbows. The cat stopped in the middle of the road, sat down, raised its back leg and began to clean its nether regions insouciantly.

'I'll pay you!' Clara raged, hurling at it all the foul words she knew. But gradually her anger gave way to dejection. It had been a long, hard day with nothing to show for it, she was bone weary, Pip was very sick and might, because of her stupidity, be in terrible danger. Overwhelmed by the misery of it all, Clara squatted on the kerb, buried her head in her hands and wept.

'What's wrong with you, young lady?'

Clara looked up in alarm. A policeman was standing over her, an elderly man by the look of his lined face and grizzled hair. 'I said, what's wrong?' he repeated as she stared at him.

'Nothin'. Nothin', guv.' She struggled to her feet, looking fearfully at the handcuffs and the cutlass in its scabbard that dangled from his belt. 'I was just goin', runnin', when that pesky cat . . .' She pointed. But the cat had gone. 'Well, there was one. Honest. He came out of that doorway and—'

'And what are you doing out at this hour, may I ask?'

'I went to look for my mum cos my brother's sick.'

'And did you find her?'

'Nah, I didn't. I asked some women and they said . . .' Clara bit her lip. Her mother had warned her to stay well clear of anyone connected with the law and never, never to tell them anything, because they would use it against you – and here she was chattering to a policeman as if he was a normal man.

'I see.' He swung his wooden truncheon ominously. 'So you've got a home, have you?'

'Course I have.'

'And where might that be?'

'Church Street.'

'Church Street. Uhm . . . that'll be just off Seven Dials. What's your name?' he asked in a kindly way.

'Clara Forbes.' Too late she realized she should not have given him her real name.

'Well, Clara, you'd best get home to your brother, hadn't you?'

'Yeh, guv, I will. Thanks,' said Clara, relieved that he was letting her go.

'And I'll come with you.'

'Nah. Nah—'

'To see you home safe and sound.'

'But—'

'Come along.' He put a firm hand on her shoulder.

15

Jem, Ned and Billy huddled in the darkest corner of a deep doorway.

'You sure a crusher won't see us?' said Ned nervously.

'Course I am,' retorted Jem. 'We can't hardly see each other, can we?'

But he had reckoned without the bullseye lantern that policemen always carried strapped to their belts and in the early hours of the morning the boys were woken by a bright beam shining into their eyes and a stern voice asking them what they thought they were doing.

Jem shot up in alarm.

'We're not vagrants, guv. We got a place to live. We got a ma and pa. We got—'

'So why're you sleeping in the street?'

'Cos we got tired. I mean, my little brother got tired and we couldn't carry him.'

'All right, I'll deal with him,' said the policeman,

throwing the still-sleeping Billy over his shoulder. 'Come on, let's get you lot home.'

'Pa'll kill us for bringin' a crusher back,' whispered Ned in his brother's ear as they hurried back to Devil's Acre with the policeman following. 'Then Ma'll wallop us black and blue.'

But when they got to Devil's Acre neither their mother nor father was there. Nor their sister Kate. The place where their caravan had stood was now empty. And their grandmother's caravan was burned to the ground.

'Gran!' they cried, looking at the pile of smouldering ashes in horror.

'So that's where your grandmother lived, was it?' asked the policeman.

'Yeh . . . Oh Lor', what if she was in it?'

'What's all the shindig?' demanded an irate neighbour, poking her head out of an upstairs window. 'Decent people're tryin' to get a bit of sleep and . . . Oh, it's you lot.' She scowled when she saw the boys. 'I might've known.'

'Are you acquainted with them, missus?' asked the policeman.

'How much?'

'D'you *know* them?'

'Know them?' she scoffed. 'Course I do. Everyone

knows them. They're the biggest load of lyin', thievin' good-for-nothin's—'

'Here, you shut your kisser!' Jem shouted, waving his fist at her.

'Enough of that or I'll run the lot of you in,' said the policeman. 'These boys say they live here. Is it true?' he asked the woman.

'They did. They lived in a filthy old caravan that was near fallin' apart. And their gran's was worse. Lucky it got burned – best thing could happen to it.'

'Never mind that,' warned the policeman, restraining Jem, who was doing his best to climb up the wall to wallop her. 'Where've they gone?'

'Don't know, don't care.'

'And what about this caravan?' The policeman pointed to the remains of Gran Perkinski's home.

'What about it?'

'Who burned it down?'

'How would I know? She probably did it herself, silly old faggot. She's as mad as a brick.'

'All right, that's enough of that, my lad,' the policeman scolded Jem, who was now hurling pieces of wood at the woman. 'Was she in it at the time?'

'Nah, worse luck. She went off with the rest of them. And good riddance, I say.' And she slammed the window shut with such force that the small piece of glass still left in one corner fell to the ground and shattered at the policeman's feet.

'Well now, I think you'd better come along with me, lads,' he said.

'Where to, guv?'

'The police station.'

'The lock-up? But why? We haven't done nothin' wrong.'

'You've got no home, you were sleeping on the street. That makes you vagrants. And vagrancy's against the law.'

'So what'll happen to us?'

'That's for the magistrate to decide, son. You'll see him in the morning.'

Jem, Ned and Billy spent the rest of that night in a police cell with a dozen or more drunken men and women, most of whom had been in fights, their faces a riot of colour from blue to purple and black, and an assortment of thieves and vagabonds. Billy slept soundly, stretched out in a corner of the dirty cell, oblivious to the incessant snoring and coughing, but his brothers stayed awake.

'Where d'you think Ma and Pa've gone, Jem?'

Ned asked for the umpteenth time, crushing a cockroach under his boot.

'I reckon they must've gone hop-pickin'. All gypsies go hop-pickin' this time of year.'

'Nah, they don't. Hop-pickin' doesn't start till September.'

'Must be pea-pickin' then.'

'Pea-pickin' doesn't start till September neither. Anyway, they'd have taken us with them.'

'Perhaps Pa got the offer of a prize fight some-where.'

'So why didn't he tell us?'

'Cos we weren't there, were we? He probably had to go right away.'

'What, with the caravan and Ma and Gran and Kate and the pig and the chickens? And why'd they burn Gran's caravan? She loved that caravan, even if it was a muck heap.'

'Nobody said *they* burned it, you stupe!'

'You mean someone else did it?'

'I'll wager it was Old Mother Perry. It's just the kind of thing that old crab would do. I'll wager she waited till they'd gone, then she crept down with a match and . . .'

'But why did Ma and Pa go, Jem? Why'd they—?'

'Look, don't keep needlin' me,' snapped Jem,

90

who was as much at a loss as his brother. 'They'll be back home in a couple of days, you'll see,' he said, trying to put on a brave face.

'But we won't, will we?' said Ned dolefully. 'We'll be doin' a couple of months' hard labour.'

16

The 'nice, quiet yard back of Hungerford Market' where the Perkinskis parked their caravan offered all the comforts they were used to in Devil's Acre — a stinking rubbish dump, piles of dung, a rain barrel full of dirty water with a layer of thick, green scum on the top, a lean-to shed that had leaned too far, a cart with no wheels and handles, numerous putrefying bodies that might once have been dogs and cats, and the usual welcoming committee of rats and mice.

'I reckon we'll be all right here,' said Pa, taking Bessie the horse out of the shafts and hitching her to a post, 'long as we lay low and don't draw attention to ourselves *by makin' a diabolical row,*' he hissed at Kate, who had started to sing 'The Banks of the Blue Moselle' in a voice that sent the cockroaches scurrying for cover.

Kate was the Perkinskis' eldest child, a pert girl of thirteen with ginger hair and more freckles on her face than on a speckled egg. Although she attracted many admirers among the coster boys and street sellers, several of whom had asked her to be their 'mate', Kate's ambition was to sing in the music halls and to this end she exercised her vocal chords morning, noon and night to the distress of everyone within earshot.

'Stop caterwaulin', Kate, and help your ma get the pig and chickens out while I make a bit of cover for them,' said Pa, picking up some of the rotting wood that remained from the lean-to shed. 'And, Gran, dry up, Lor's sake!' he snapped at the old woman, who was moaning and groaning because she had left her caravan and all her magic potions and lotions behind.

'But what'll I do without them, Bert?' she whined. 'I can't work no more. I can't do nothin'. I—'

'You can get a fire goin' for some hot water,' said Pa pragmatically. 'I could do with somethin' to wet my whistle.'

'You should stay in the caravan, Bert. You got to hide,' said Ma, looking anxiously over her shoulder. 'It only takes the wrong pair of eyes to see you and you're done for.'

'How long we got to stay here, Ma?' demanded

Kate, who resented having to leave Devil's Acre and her job at the Dog and Bacon.

'Till Killer Kelly stops lookin' for your pa.'

'And when'll that be?'

'Never,' said Ma with a shudder. 'That brute'll never give up.'

17

The policeman kept a tight hold of Clara as he took her back to the lodging house in Church Street. The girl could feel a hundred eyes boring into them as they walked through the squalid streets and hear the muttered curses from disembodied voices in dark doorways and courtyards.

The policeman heard them too.

'That you, Bob Miles?' he demanded, shining his lantern up an alleyway. 'What are you creeping round there for?'

'What am I doin' wrong, Mr Ross?' whined a villainous-looking youth, appearing at the end of the alley.

'I'll let you know pretty quick if you don't hook it! You too, Mr Click,' said the policeman as an even wickeder face appeared alongside the first. 'Hook it, the pair of you, or I'll take you down to the lock-up.'

Policemen rarely penetrated the heart of London's

most dangerous slum, and then only in twos or threes, their night sticks at the ready, but Constable Ross was well known in the rookeries and despite their hatred of the police people felt a grudging respect for a man who had the courage to walk through such a dangerous neighbourhood alone, and at night.

'This where you live?' he asked when Clara stopped in front of a narrow house with no door.

She nodded.

'Go on, then.'

She began to climb the rotting staircase and was unnerved to discover the man close behind her.

'You don't need to come up,' she said. 'I'm all right now.'

'I'll take you to your room,' he said in a voice that brooked no opposition.

Clara shrugged. She was home, among her own people, safe. He couldn't – wouldn't – try to arrest her. Would he?

When they reached the room on the top floor Constable Ross flashed his bullseye lantern around it, illuminating the filthy floorboards, the crumbling walls, the broken windows stuffed with paper, the foul-smelling slop bucket in the middle. Immediately the inert bodies on the floor sprang to life. When they saw the tall, blue-suited figure standing in the doorway they scrambled away, cringing, shielding their faces from the light. One cried, 'I've not done nothin' wrong, guv,' and another made a bolt for it down the stairs.

'You little varmint, bringin' a crusher back here,' someone muttered in Clara's ear. 'You wait till he's gone, I'll . . .'

But the girl neither heard nor cared about the threat. She was looking for her brother.

'Where's the woman that took Pip?' she said, running round the room and peering anxiously into every face. 'Where is she?' she cried in mounting alarm. 'Where's that woman? Where's Pip?' Her voice rose to a scream.

'You know anything about this?' demanded Constable Ross as the lodgers huddled against the walls.

They shook their heads.

'Do you know this girl?'

They stared at the floor. There was always some fracas in the rookeries at night, a murder, a mugging, a kidnap. It was best to shake your head, stare at the floor, claim you knew nothing about it.

'But I . . . I was here. You saw me. You heard Pip

cryin'. *You* —' she rounded on the drunkard — 'you wanted to give him some of your gin.'

'Liar!' he scowled at her. 'I don't know what she's talkin' about, guv,' he said to the policeman in a grovelling voice. 'I never seen her before. I never seen no baby neither.'

Clara stared at him aghast, her face ashen in the lamplight. She opened her mouth to say something, but try as she might only a gasping, gurgling sound came out.

'All right, my treasure,' said Constable Ross, lifting her gently and putting her over his shoulder. 'You'd best come with me.'

18

Soon after dawn Jem, Ned and Billy were bundled into the back of a police cart and driven to a large, imposing building that Jem immediately recognized as the court house.

Many people were waiting in the courtyard and a stout, officious man with a huge bunch of keys in his hand pushed the boys to the end of the line and instructed them to stand still and be quiet until their names were called.

'Who's he?' asked Billy, staring at the keys the man swung back and forth till they almost mesmerized him.

'I am Her Majesty's jailer,' said the man.

'D'you know who the beak is, guv?' Jem asked him.

'I imagine you are referrin' to the magistrate,' said the jailer, frowning down his nose at the boy. 'For your information, his name is Mr Flynn.'

'Never heard of him,' said Jem.

'Never heard of Flynn the Flogger?' muttered a shifty-eyed boy standing next to him. 'You should count yourself lucky. He gave me twenty lashes last time. I couldn't sit down for weeks.'

'What did you do?' asked Jem.

'I stood up.'

'I mean, why did he give you fifty lashes?'

'Cos I was caught sleepin' in a shop doorway.'

'Oh Lor,' muttered Ned.

'Right, you three,' shouted the jailer after a while, 'you're next.'

'Now remember, Ned, let me do all the talkin'. And, Billy, you hold your jaw too. Don't go upsettin' the beak, you hear?' said Jem as they were pushed into a small, gloomy office.

'Right, get in there,' said the jailer, pointing to a wooden pen in one corner, 'and bow to the bar.'

'What bar?' cried Billy, in his high-pitched voice. 'I don't see no bar. I can't see nothin'.'

'Give the child a stool to stand on,' said the clerk of the court.

A stool was produced and Billy lifted on to it so that he could see over the top of the pen.

'Who's he?' He pointed at an elderly man sitting at a desk behind a bar at the far end of the room.

'I am the presiding magistrate,' said the man,

looking at Billy with eyes as frosty as a January morning.

'Oh, right.' Billy beamed at him. 'Hello, Mr Flogger.'

Jem stifled a groan and Ned covered his face with trembling hands.

'My name is Mr Flynn,' said the magistrate stiffly, 'but you will address me as Your Honour. Officer —' he turned to the clerk — 'with what are these boys charged?'

'Vagrancy, Your Honour.'

'Where is the constable who arrested them?'

'He is here, Your Honour. It's Constable Murray.'

'Very well, swear him.'

Constable Murray stepped into the witness box, put his hand on the Bible and swore to tell the truth and then told the magistrate in a ponderous voice how he had discovered Jem, Ned and Billy in a shop doorway in the early hours of the morning.

'And they were behaving badly, I imagine, fighting and shouting, disturbing the peace?' said Flynn, leaning towards him.

'No, Your Honour, they were not. As a matter of fact they were all dormant.'

'What?'

'Asleep.'

'But they tried to run away when you arrested them?'

'No, Your Honour, they were most quiescent.'

'What?'

'They came quietly.'

'Oh.' If Flynn had been capable of expressing any emotion it would have been one of disappointment.

'Do they have a home? parents?'

'No, Your Honour. They—'

'Yeh, we do,' Jem interrupted him. 'We got a ma and pa and—'

'Be quiet, boy!' Flynn said sharply. 'Pray continue, Constable Murray.'

'They conducted me to Devil's Acre, a disreputable area in close proximity to the Abbey in the district of Westminster—'

'Yes, yes, I know where it is,' said Flynn testily. 'Get on!'

'They gave me to understand that they had been residin' there for some considerable time,' said the constable, who seemed to think it necessary to address the magistrate in a very pompous way. 'However, when we arrived upon the scene, there appeared to be nobody present, Your Honour. A neighbour by the name of Mrs Adelaide Perry—'

'A right old hag,' muttered Jem. 'Her tongue's worn to a stub with chatterin'.'

'I won't warn you again!' snapped Flynn, glaring at him.

'Mrs Perry informed me that the boys' parents had indeed been living there but that they had vacated the vicinity, Your Honour.'

'So they abandoned their children?'

'That would appear to be the case, Your Honour.'

'Disgraceful,' muttered Flynn, frowning at Jem, Ned and Billy as if it was their fault. 'How old are they?'

'How old are you?' asked the clerk.

'Eleven,' said Jem. 'And Ned's ten. And Billy's goin' on six.'

'Hmm, too young for prison . . . yet,' said Flynn regretfully. 'I therefore propose to commit them to the workhouse.'

'The workhouse?' cried Jem and Ned, aghast, for they knew all about the place where paupers went, the homeless and hopeless, the starving and sick people with no one to care for them and no energy or will to care for themselves.

'Nah, nah, don't send us there, Your Honour. Please!' Ned begged him. 'Give us twenty lashes, ship us to Australie, but don't send us to the work-house.'

'Silence!' thundered Flynn, half rising from his seat in his agitation. 'You should be grateful that I am committing you to a place where you will be fed, clothed and well cared for. Though I dare say you don't deserve it.'

'But—'

'Another word from you, boy, and you will be flogged and *then* sent to the workhouse!'

'Which house do you recommend, Your Honour?' asked the clerk of the court.

'Westminster.'

'The Westminster Union has no vacancies, Your Honour.'

'Oh, very well, send them to the Strand Workhouse. Mr Blood runs an excellent establish-ment. They'll come to no harm there.'

19

Ma was distraught.

'The boys should've been here ages ago,' she said, pacing up and down the yard wringing her hands. 'They should've been here by now.'

'Don't fret, Ma, they probably got lost. You know what Ned's like. He can't hardly find his way out of bed. And as for Billy, I reckon a pork pie's got more brains than him,' Kate said comfortingly.

'But Jem's up to snuff,' Ma protested. 'He'd have got his brothers here all right, unless . . . oh Lor'!' She stopped dead, her eyes wide with fear as a terrible thought struck her.

'Unless what, Ma?'

'Unless Killer Kelly went to Devil's Acre last night and found the boys there and . . . Where're you goin', Bert?' Her voice rose shrilly as Pa appeared at the door of the caravan with his cap on.

'I'm goin' to look for them. Kate's right, they probably got lost – or Jem's up to one of his dodges,' he chuckled, trying to sound unconcerned so as not to upset Ma even more, although in his heart he was as anxious as she was.

'You off your chump?' Ma grabbed his arm. 'You want to make it easier for Killer Kelly to find you?'

'Yeh.' Gran nodded. 'Half London knows your ugly mug, Bert. Someone'd see you before you got to the bottom of the street, then Killer Kelly'd get wind of it and—'

'And I'll lose you as well as my boys,' said Ma, tears welling up in her eyes.

'But I got to do somethin', my ducky,' said Pa. 'I can't just sit here, knowin' Jem, Ned and Billy are—'

'I'll go and find them,' said Ma, ramming her old boater on her head and tucking her straggly grey hair under it.

'But, Liza—'

'Don't argufy, Bert. I'm goin'.'

'Well, I'm not lettin' you go alone and there's an end to it.'

'I'll go with her, Bert,' said Gran.

'Nah, you won't,' said Ma. 'I'll waste all my time waitin' for you to catch up. I'll take Kate.'

'Nah!' cried the girl, backing away.

'Kate, go with your ma,' said Pa sternly.

'But, Pa—'

'I'm not lettin' your ma go on her own. If you won't go with her, I will.'

'Oh all right,' Kate muttered.

'Good girl,' said Pa, giving her a hug. 'And the two of you,' he added, putting an arm around Ma's shoulders, 'you be careful. Don't do nothin' silly.'

20

'Yet another child abandoned by its parents? That's the fourth this morning,' Flynn said in an exasperated voice. 'Have these wretched people no sense of responsibility? Must you and I,' he addressed himself to the clerk of the court, 'always be the ones to pay for the upkeep of their unwanted offspring?'

The clerk, who was a more compassionate man than the magistrate, bowed his head and made some non-committal remark. But Flynn's question had been rhetorical. He neither wanted nor expected a reply. He had long ago made up his mind that the unending line of shabby, dejected people who shuffled past him each morning deliberately chose to lead such dismal lives.

'Well, have you anything to say for yourself?' he barked at Clara.

The girl cut a drab figure in her battered straw hat, patched skirt, down-at-heel boots and bits of string threaded through the holes in her earlobes, as had many other small girls, in the belief that it would improve her eyesight. But she stood up straight and looked at the magistrate defiantly with her bright, button eyes.

'So you won't speak, eh? Dumb insolence. The punishment for that is—'

'With respect, Your Honour,' the clerk interrupted him, 'despite repeated questioning on our part, the child has not responded. I humbly submit, therefore, that the shock brought on by her misfortune has rendered her incapable of speech.'

'Oh very well, send her to the Westminster Union.'

'But the Westminster Union is—'

'Yes, yes, yes. Then she must go to the Strand Workhouse. Mr and Mrs Blood will take good care of her.'

21

The Strand Workhouse was more like a prison than a refuge for the sick and homeless. A grim, four-storey building with grey walls and tiny windows, its forbidding appearance struck terror into the hearts of everyone who passed.

After a surly reception from the porter at the gate, Jem, Ned and Billy were shown into a receiving ward where a shrewish clerk wrote their names, ages and last known address in a large ledger, frequently dipping his quill pen into an inkstand.

'We're not stayin' here,' said Jem. 'We got to get back to our ma and pa. They'll be worryin' about us.'

'And where are they?' asked the clerk, peering at him over silver-rimmed spectacles.

'They . . . er . . . they gone away. They gone to foreign parts.'

'Foreign parts?' the clerk smirked. 'Foreign parts? Well, well. Which foreign parts?'

Since Jem had never been further than Walworth he had no idea where those who could afford the luxury of travel went, but he did remember his father telling him where gypsies came from.

'Egypt,' he said.

'Egypt?' Another smirk. 'They must be made of money, your parents.'

'They are,' Jem nodded. 'They're dirty rich.'

'And that is why they live in a dilapidated caravan in a slum, no doubt?'

'A *what* caravan?'

'Let us stop this nonsense,' said the clerk waspishly. 'You will stay here until—'

'You can't keep us here,' Jem shouted him down. 'You can't keep nobody in the workhouse if they want to leave.'

'That only applies to inmates over the age of twelve.'

'Oh. Oh well, that's all right, cos I am.'

'You told me you were eleven. And your birthday —' the clerk consulted the ledger — 'is not until December.'

'Did I say that?' Jem laughed nervously. 'I meant today.'

'Yeh, it's my birthday today too,' said Ned.

'And mine,' added Billy.

'And I suppose you're all twelve years old,' said the clerk.

The boys nodded.

'Enough!' The clerk slammed the ledger shut. 'Mrs Murphy,' he called to an orderly waiting outside, 'take these three to Dr Robson.'

'Follow me,' she said with a curt nod of the head.

The workhouse doctor was a young man with a kinder face than the porter, clerk or orderly and he examined Jem, Ned and Billy carefully, listening to their heart and lungs with his stethoscope.

'Have you ever suffered from a contagious illness?' he asked.

'What's that mean?'

'Contagious means that it can be passed from one person to another. I am referring to dangerous diseases, like typhus, cholera or smallpox.'

Jem narrowed his eyes. 'You . . . er . . . you wouldn't want nothin' like that in here, would you, guv?' he said.

'Certainly not. There are so many weak, hungry people in this institution they would die within the day.'

'Ah.' Jem nodded. 'Well, to be honest with you, I've got typhus.'

'And I've got cholera,' said Ned.

'And I've got small spots,' added Billy.

Dr Robson put a hand over his mouth to hide a smile. 'My lads,' he said, 'if you had those diseases you would be close to death.'

'Oh, we are, aren't we?' Jem turned to his brothers.

'Yeh.' Ned nodded. 'Matter of fact –' he gestured towards Billy, who was gazing into space with his usual vacant expression – 'I reckon he's already there.'

The doctor's smile became a chuckle and picking up a hand bell on his desk he rang it.

'Mr Jackson,' he said to the thuggish orderly who appeared in answer to his summons. 'I give these new inmates into your care, and may God have mercy on the poor wretches,' he muttered when the man was out of earshot.

'Are we goin' to have dinner now?' asked Billy as the orderly led them across an unpaved courtyard inches deep in muck.

'Not till you've had a wash,' he said, pushing them through a door into the bath-house.

Jem, Ned and Billy had never seen a bath-house before, so they had no idea that the large pool in which half a dozen men were scrubbing and splashing water over themselves was not an ordinary one.

'Take off all your clothes,' instructed the orderly, 'and leave them on the floor over there. Come on, hurry up,' he snapped as the boys looked at each other doubtfully.

'I don't need a wash,' said Billy, cringing. 'I'm clean.'

'You're about as clean as a dunghill. I could smell you a mile off. Now get in and be sharp about it.'

There was a brief altercation when Ned was parted from his catapult – 'But it's a crack one, best I ever made,' he cried as the orderly wrenched it from his hand – and Jem refused to get in the water unless he kept his wideawake on. 'But I never take it off, never!' he protested, clinging to it with both hands.

'It'd make a good basin,' said one of the men in the bath. And before Jem could stop him he had snatched the hat, filled it with water, poured it over his head and passed it on to the next man.

Jem ranted and raved, claiming they had stolen his property and he'd call the police. But this threat was greeted with bellows of laughter.

'And how're you goin' to *call* them? Stand on the roof and holler, are you?'

Even the orderly enjoyed the joke. 'No crushers'd ever dare come in here,' he chuckled. 'We'd skin 'em alive.'

'Look what you done,' Jem cried in despair when his limp, sodden hat was finally returned to him. 'You ruined it.'

'You won't be needin' it no more, anyway,' said the orderly, throwing it on the pile of dirty clothes. 'Now get in that bath and be sharp about it.' And he handed Jem a large brush with fierce bristles.

The water was pleasantly cool after the scorching sunshine but since several dozen extremely dirty men and boys had already washed themselves in it, it had taken on the colour and consistency of mushroom soup.

'Don't just stand there,' shouted the orderly. 'Scrub yourselves. Go on! You're not comin' out till you're red as a beetroot's bottom.'

After a few minutes of vigorous scrubbing the boys' skins had turned from dark grey to pale grey to white to pink and finally the required shade of red.

'That's more like it,' said the orderly. 'You can get out now. And put these on.' He handed each of them a short jacket and trousers which had been worn by so many children over the years their

115

original colour, which might have been blue, had taken on a greyish black hue. To add to the boys' discomfort, the drab clothes were made of a coarse fabric known as fustian, which felt like a thick hairy blanket.

'And here's your boots,' said the orderly, handing each of them a pair of hobnailed boots tipped with iron.

'Crikey!' exclaimed Jem. 'They're so heavy I can't hardly lift them. Why can't I wear my own boots?'

'You'll get your own gear back when you leave – *if* you leave, which I doubt,' said the orderly with a wolfish grin. 'Right, now you're goin' to have a haircut.'

'Mine don't need cuttin',' said Ned, who was rather fond of the greasy spikes that stuck up all over his head.

'You got to have the regulation cut.'

'What's that?'

'You'll see.'

Ned and Billy sat quietly while the orderly cropped their hair to within an inch of their scalp. But he was no hairdresser and the result was hideous.

'Crimes, you look a right couple of ninnies,'

sniggered Jem. 'You got long bits of hair right next to bald patches. Oy, you're not doin' that to me,' he cried as the orderly approached him, chinking the shears ominously. 'You come near me with them and I'll . . .'

It took three men to hold him down while the orderly gave him the workhouse haircut, or his own even uglier version of it.

'Right,' said the man, standing back to admire his handiwork, 'let's go.'

'We goin' to have dinner now?' cried Billy.

'Nah, you got to see Mr Blood first.'

'Who's he?'

'The master of this workhouse. Now come on.' And gesturing to them to follow him, he crossed the yard, climbed a narrow flight of stairs and stopped outside the apartment where Blood lived with his wife and son.

'Stand up straight and look lively,' he snapped as the boys shuffled along, making slow progress in their heavy boots. 'And don't speak till you're spoken to. The master doesn't like clack boxes.'

Someone was playing the piano, banging the keys in a confident but tuneless way, but the noise stopped when the orderly tapped on the door.

'Come!' shouted a voice.

Whether the orderly was rather deaf or momentarily distracted by the sight of two men beating each other to a pulp in the yard below is difficult to say, but he tapped on the door again.

'I said, COME!' The voice rose to a bellow.

This had a dramatic effect on the orderly, for he immediately stopped being a swaggering bully and metamorphosed into a coward quaking at the sound of his master's voice.

'Go on!' he hissed, opening the door. 'Go on!'

22

'You go up the Strand and I'll go back to Devil's Acre and see if that old cat Perry knows anythin',' Ma said as she and Kate hurried through the streets. 'I'll meet you in the Square in a while. And, Kate,' Ma added sternly, 'don't waste time. Keep remindin' yourself you're supposed to be lookin' for Jem, Ned and Billy, not canoodlin' with boys.'

The Strand was one of London's busiest thoroughfares and on that day as on any other, with the exception of Sunday when everything ground to a halt, it was packed with people and a colourful assortment of street musicians, clowns, acrobats and sandwich-board men to entertain and inform them.

Kate started at the Aldwych and worked her way towards Trafalgar Square, asking everyone who might have known her brothers if they had seen them that morning.

'Nah, I haven't,' said a man standing at the

corner of Bull Inn Court, pausing in the middle of a lusty rendition of 'The Tartar Drum', 'but I saw them yesterday, worse luck. I was singin' a sentimental song called "Isle of Beauty" – d'you know it, miss? Oh, it's a real tear jerker and no mistake. Some of the ladies were dabbin' at their cheeks and reachin' for their purses when them three pesky brothers of yours came along and started howlin' like a dog with a thorn up its bum. Ruined it for me, they did. If I ever get my hands on them . . .'

'Oh, I know them right enough, they were here day before yesterday,' said a man who was grinding out a waltz on his barrel organ. 'The littl'un tried to steal peanuts from Queenie,' he pointed at a tiny monkey in a red suit with a ruff collar and pantaloons, who was dancing to the music. 'I'm learnin' her to bite Billy whenever she sees him,' he said. And the monkey bared her teeth and jumped up and down screaming, as if just hearing the boy's name sent her into a paroxysm of rage.

By the time Kate reached Trafalgar Square Ma was already there, the worry lines etched even more deeply in her tired face.

'Well?' she called anxiously, running towards her daughter.

'Nah, nobody's seen them today, Ma. Not in the Strand, anyway.'

Ma's shoulders sagged.

'Did you see Old Mother Perry?' said Kate.

'Nah, I bawled my head off but she didn't hear me. I reckon she was up in her room stirrin' a bucket of poison with her tongue.'

'What about Spud?'

'Spud?' Ma spat out the name as if it was snake venom. 'That half-baked, knocker-faced blockhead said he came out of the pub last night a bit worse for wear and had an argument with a brick wall and ended up with his brains all over the road – not that he's got any,' said Ma disparagingly. 'So by the time he dragged himself back to Devil's Acre the boys must've come and gone, so they didn't get our message. I tell you, Kate, if Spud hadn't been half dead already I'd have killed him. I've said to your pa time and time again we shouldn't let that good-for-nothin' lush stay in our pigsty. He only pays a penny a week rent and the pig doesn't like him and—'

'Ma,' Kate interrupted her mother's tirade against their unfortunate lodger, 'did you get them potions of Gran's like she asked?'

'Nah, I couldn't.'

'Why not?'

'Cos her caravan's burned.'

'*Burned?*'

'To the ground. Nothin' left of it but a pile of ashes, and this —' Ma held up a glass ball — 'Gran's crystal.'

Kate's eyes nearly started from her head. 'Lawks a mercy, Ma,' she exclaimed. 'Whoever'd do a horrible thing like that?'

'Killer Kelly,' said Ma grimly. 'I reckon he came lookin' for Pa and when he didn't find him he burned Gran's caravan thinkin' it was ours. He's a bitter man, full of revenge.'

'Gran'll tear him limb from limb when she finds out.'

'Don't be a goosecap, Kate,' Ma chided her. 'He could tear her limb from limb with one hand tied behind his back. Nah, make that both hands. Anyway, I got more important things to worry about than Gran's caravan. I've got to find my boys. Oy, you,' she shouted at a juggler balancing an umbrella on his nose while he tossed half a dozen cups and plates in the air, 'you seen three boys in the Square this mornin'?'

'Three boys?' scoffed the man, pausing in his act.

'I seen three hundred, more like three thousand, and all of them pesky little varmints.'

'I'm lookin' for my sons, Jem, Ned and Billy.'

'Oh them – the worst of the lot. One's a real villain in the makin'—'

'That'll be Jem,' said Ma proudly.

'He crept up behind me, the saucebox, and tickled my armpits, made me drop all my cups and plates. I had to go and buy some more. I told him if he ever comes near me again . . .' He brandished his umbrella like a cosh.

'But where did they go after that?' said Ma.

'Over there.' He pointed at the pavement in front of St-Martin-in-the-Fields. 'I saw them nick a broom off a poor little crossin' sweeper. But they got their comeuppance all right.' He grinned. 'They were copped.'

'Oh blimey,' Ma groaned, 'not again. Pa'll go off his nut if he has to pay another fine.'

'Nah, it wasn't a crusher that copped them. It was Captain.'

'And who the devil's Captain?'

'He's a bigwig in the Crossin' Sweepers' Association.'

'I don't care if he's a king-wig, he's got no right

to cop my boys,' said Ma indignantly. 'Where's he taken them?'

'To court.'

'Court? You must be kiddin'.'

'Nah, they got a proper court.'

'And where is this crossin' sweepers' court?'

'In their paddin' ken.'

'And where's that?'

'How should I know? You'd best ask Captain. He's over there, leanin' on Nelson,' said the man, indicating the column in the middle of the Square. And balancing the umbrella on his nose, he started juggling his plates and cups again.

23

Jem was first to enter the workmaster's parlour and it took a moment or two for his eyes to adjust to the darkness. Like many a reception room in a Victorian house it was decorated in oppressive shades of maroon, dark green and brown with heavy curtains and a jungle of tall plants blocking the light from the windows.

A profusion of ornaments, glass domes of waxed fruit, stuffed animals and birds, goblets, statuettes, candlesticks, vases, lamps and caskets covered the dresser, writing desk, occasional tables, stands and shelves, and photographs, paintings, pieces of tapestry, wood carvings and pictures made out of dried flowers and shells covered every inch of the walls.

A large, overstuffed chair stood on each side of the ornate fireplace with its brass fender, coal scuttle and tongs and above it was a large gilt mirror in which was reflected a woman sitting at an upright piano, her hands suspended over the keys.

Jem spun round. 'Crimes!' he exclaimed.

Mrs Blood invariably had this effect on people when they met her for the first time. Perhaps they expected a workhouse master's wife to be a trifle more discreet, perhaps a tad more conservative, if not downright plain and dowdy. Not Mrs Blood. She may have lived in a workhouse but in her heart she was a grande dame, a lady of fashion, her hennaed curls piled under a jaunty little bonnet copiously decorated with flowers and feathers, a wide velvet band with coloured beads around her fleshy neck, her stout body corseted so tightly into a poplin gown that her plump breasts threatened to plop over the top of her bodice with every breath she took.

Next to her, his huge head thrust forward on a bull-like neck, stood a short, powerfully built man with a swarthy skin. His nose was broad and flat with large, flaring nostrils, his mouth so thin he seemed to have no lips. Beneath the prominent ridge of his eyebrows a pair of black beady eyes watched the three boys with the uncomprehending suspicion of a great ape. But it was his hair that made Jem mutter, 'Crimes!' yet again, a mass of

black bristles that grew low on his neck and forehead, sprouted from his nose and ears and covered
his arms and hands.

'I brought these new inmates for you to see, sir,'
said the orderly, thrusting the boys towards him.

'I'll leave you, Mr Blood,' said his wife, closing
the lid of the piano and getting to her feet. 'Playin'
has quite fatigued me. I think I'll retire to my
room.' And she swept out, waving Jem, Ned and
Billy aside with an imperious gesture.

The master stood for a while, his shoulders
hunched forward, his legs splayed wide, his huge
hands hanging loosely by his side, glaring at the
boys.

'Paupers,' he said at last, his voice full of con-
tempt. 'More snivellin' cadgers too lazy to work.
Well, don't think you're goin' to have a soft life
here, my lads,' he said, wagging a finger at them.
'Don't think you can stuff your bellies and lay about
doin' nothin' just because you've wormed your way
into the workhouse.'

'But we didn't—' began Jem.

'Hold your tongue!' roared Blood, and he
smacked Jem on the side of the head so hard the boy
rocked back and would have fallen if Ned hadn't

 127

caught him. 'I'll tell you when you can speak. Now where was I, Mr Jackson?' He turned to the orderly.

'These boys were wormin' their way into the workhouse, sir,' said the orderly, knotting his hands together under his chin and giving a little half-bow.

'Now listen, you three, you'll be all square provided you obey the rules,' said Blood, bending so close they could smell the gin on his breath. 'And the rules are simple — work hard, act proper and keep your mouths tight shut — that means no talkin' in the corridors or bed wards or dinin' hall. If you break the rules, you'll regret it. I got no time for snivellin' little faggots that break the rules. I can get real nasty. D'you get my meanin'?'

The boys nodded.

'I said, D'YOU GET MY MEANIN'?' Blood bellowed.

'Yeh,' said Ned, looking nervously at Jem, who was staring at the floor, a stubborn expression on his face.

'Yeh, what?' Blood said.

'Yeh, we get your meanin'.'

'And what else?' Blood began to tap his foot, which was clearly an ominous sign because the orderly backed towards the door, cringing.

'AND WHAT ELSE?' screeched Blood, raising his fist to hit Ned.

'Yeh, we get your meanin', *sir*,' muttered Jem.

'Good.' Blood looked at him approvingly. 'I'm pleased to see one of you's got manners. And another thing: don't try to run away. I don't want you to stay here – nobody does, you're just wastin' the money of decent, God-fearin', hard-workin' people – but you got to stay till you're twelve. That's the law. So if you make a bolt for it, I'll come after you. And I'll bring you back. I always bring bolters back. And when I do . . .' Blood rubbed his hands, clearly relishing the punishment he inflicted on boys who tried to escape. 'Right, Mr Jackson,' he said to the orderly, 'take them away and show them their accommodations.'

The boys' 'accommodations' was a long room with a low ceiling blackened by smoke. There were no chairs, no tables, nothing but rotting floorboards to sit on and bare brick walls covered with mould to look at.

'This is the day ward,' said the orderly, pushing Jem and Ned in. 'The other kids'll be back in a minute. Come on,' he said to Billy, 'you're comin' with me.'

'Oy, where you takin' him?' said Jem.

'He's goin' to the infants' ward.'

'What's infants?'

'Babies.'

'I'm not a baby,' protested Billy.

'Nah, you're not. And you're stayin' with us,' said Jem, grabbing his little brother and pulling him back.

'This ward's only for juveniles — that's boys seven to fifteen. This kid's goin' to the infants' ward whether you like it or not.' And the orderly swung his arm in a wide arc, knocking Jem off his feet, and dragged a screaming Billy away.

Jem hit the floor with such force he was knocked unconscious for a moment and when he came to Ned was kneeling by his side, his eyes shiny with terror.

'You all right, Jem? You all right? You all right?' he asked over and over.

'I think he's broken my jaw,' mumbled Jem, touching it gingerly. 'Yeh,' he winced, 'I can't feel it. It's gone all funny.'

'Nah, it can't be broken, else you couldn't talk. Remember when Spud had a set-to with that bloke in the Dog'n Bacon? Gave him a right stockdollager, he did – broke his jaw. Spud couldn't hardly say a word for weeks.'

'What happened to Billy?' said Jem, getting slowly to his feet.

'That bloke took him. I could hear him screamin' blue murder, poor little nipper.' Ned swallowed hard. 'We got to get him back, Jem.'

'Yeh, course we will. We'll find him and then we'll get out of this place.'

'How?'

Jem looked at the stout door with its locks and bolts and the small windows set so high in the wall they were impossible to reach.

'They can't keep us in here forever. It's just a matter of waitin' for the right opportunity. Hey up, looks as if someone's comin',' he said as a key grated in the lock.

The door of the ward opened and sixty or seventy boys trooped in, all dressed in the same drab uniform as Jem and Ned, their hair mercilessly cropped so that they looked like young convicts.

As thin as broom handles, with hollow cheeks and eyes sunk deep into their sockets, they barely glanced at the brothers, walking past them like zombies and flopping on to the floor, their backs against the damp walls. And there they stayed, sunk in misery and despair, their shoulders slumped, their slack mouths hanging open, moving only to wipe their red-raw eyes now and then with a dirty rag.

After a while one of them got up and strolled over. A boy of about Jem's age with black curly hair and a face that would have been very round if he'd had enough to eat, he stared at the brothers keenly as if they were exhibits in a glass case.

'What you lookin' at?' demanded Jem, bristling.

'You,' came the reply. 'Just arrived?'

'Yeh.'

'Been in before?'

'Nah.'

'What're your names?'

'Who's askin'?'

'My name's Doug.'

'I'm Jem and he's Ned.'

'You need to know anythin', you ask me.' The boy put his hands on his hips and rocked back and forth on his hobnailed boots. 'I know everythin' about this place, everythin'.'

'Oh yeh?' said Jem, resenting the boy's bossy manner. 'How come you know so much?'

'Cos every time my dad gets a job he takes us out of here, but he's got somethin' wrong with his leg.

It hurts so much he can't hardly walk on it let alone work, so he brings us back in here. I reckon we been in and out about forty times. All my sisters were born in this place.'

'So where's your pa now?'

'In the men's ward, of course. And my mum's in the women's. And my sisters – I got six of them, worse luck – are in the girls' ward. Only I don't hardly see them cos it isn't allowed.'

'We got a brother, Billy, in the infants' ward,' said Ned.

'We're goin' to get him out,' said Jem.

Doug gave a hollow laugh. 'Don't be sappy. If Blood catches you anywhere near the infants' ward he'll flog the skin off your back.'

'Then I won't let him catch me, will I?'

'You got to be up to snuff to get the better of Blood.' Doug lowered his voice and leaned towards Jem and Ned. 'He used to be a policeman. Took bribes. Still does. Did you see his rooms? Like Buckin'ham Palace, aren't they? That's cos people bribe him to give them the contracts for food and stuff for this place. He's dirty rich. Rollin' in it. A right villain too. He got a job as porter here, then taskmaster. There was a nice old couple ran this place, but Blood did a favour for the Guardians

when he was a crusher, you know what I mean –'
Doug winked – 'so they kicked out the old'uns and
gave him the job. Everythin' changed then. He's a
dangerous bloke, Blood.'

'So why does your pa keep bringin' you back
here?' asked Jem.

The boy shrugged. 'No place else to go.'

24

'Say somethin', damn you!' Blood shouted at Clara. 'If you don't open your mouth I'm goin' to—'

'Mr Blood, *please*.' His wife picked up her reticule and took out a phial of smelling salts which she wafted delicately under her podgy nose. 'You're hurtin' my head somethin' awful.'

'I'm sorry, dearest. I do beg your pardon,' said the master, bending over her with a concerned expression.

'May I make a suggestion, Mr Blood?'

'Of course, dearest. What is it?'

'Now that Nell has . . . er . . . departed, I am in need of a maid. I think this girl will make an excellent replacement. She looks quite strong. Well –' she hesitated, running her eye over Clara's thin body – 'stronger than most of the other girls here anyway. And she can't speak. Such a blessin', Mr Blood. Nell fair got on my nerves with her chatterin'. What's this one's name?'

'Clara Forbes.'

'Clara? Oh no.' Mrs Blood shook her head till her chins wobbled. 'I think we should call her Polly.'

'Why, dearest?' said Blood, looking perplexed.

'Polly Parrot, Mr Blood, cos she never stops talkin'.'

The master clearly thought this was the funniest joke he had ever heard and he had to hold his sides for fear he would split in two laughing. But the scornful expression on Clara's face quickly turned his amusement to anger.

'Go on, get out!' he growled, pushing her towards the door. 'And you'd better work like a navvy for Mrs Blood or I'll break every bone in your body.'

25

'He's got that look about him,' said Ma, nodding at Captain as he swaggered back and forth, sweeping his crossing, 'like somebody who thinks he's some-body.' She sniffed. 'Well, I'll soon cut him down to size. I'm goin' to give him a piece of my mind.'

'Hold hard, Ma!' Kate pulled her back. 'You go at him like sticks a-breakin' and he won't tell you nothin'. We'd best bide our time, then follow him when he goes. Sure as life he'll lead us back to the paddin' ken where him and the other sweepers live and we'll find Jem, Ned and Billy.'

'Mm, reckon you're right, my tulip,' agreed Ma. And she and Kate wandered around the Square pre-tending to beg for money while keeping a close eye on Captain.

'He's havin' a bad mornin',' Ma said after an hour or so. 'Nobody's givin' him nothin'. He's lookin' real glumpish about it. Oh, oh look, now he's given up,' she said as Captain slung his broom over his shoulder and strode away.

'Don't get too close to him, Ma,' Kate warned her as she scurried after the boy. 'They're a leery lot them crossin' sweepers and if he thinks you're followin' him he'll scarper.'

Ma slowed down and she and Kate followed Captain at a discreet distance.

'Oh crimes,' muttered Kate, clutching her mother's arm as Captain went up St Martin's Lane and turned into Castle Street, 'He's goin' into Seven Dials.'

Ma swallowed hard. Seven Dials was one of the most dangerous rookeries in London. Even Pa, a prize fighter, wouldn't go there. 'But I've got to find my boys,' she said. 'Tell you what, you stay here, Kate, and I'll—'

'Nah.'

'But—'

'Nah, I'm comin' with you, Ma.'

'Good girl.' Ma gave her a kiss on the cheek. 'Come on then, quick, before we lose him.'

Even though Ma and Kate stayed well back, hiding behind other people or dodging into doorways, Captain stopped now and then and turned, as if he sensed their presence.

'He's a sharp one and no mistake,' muttered Ma admiringly. 'Ah, look, look, that's where he lives,' she said, as the boy turned into Great White Lion Street. 'He's goin' into that house. Come on!'

Captain and Goose were in the kitchen trying to cadge a piece of bread off Mother Bailey when Ma and Kate peered cautiously round the door.

'D'you want a lodgin' for the night, my lovelies?' the landlady called to them. 'I got a couple of places in a nice room on the first floor. Only threepence for the two of you.'

'I might do,' said Ma, feigning nonchalance. 'I'll have to see it first, though.'

'What for?' Mother Bailey narrowed her eyes. 'It's just a room, same as any other – a floor, a ceilin', four walls.'

'It's cos of my girl.' Ma put an arm around Kate's shoulder. 'She gets very chesty if she doesn't get enough air, don't you, my tulip?' she said, squeezing her daughter so hard the girl gasped and spluttered.

'Here, she hasn't got consumption, has she?' cried the landlady in alarm.

'Does she look it?' laughed Ma, pointing at Kate's freckled cheeks.

'Oh, all right. Come on up, if you must. And you two –' Mother Bailey wagged a finger at Captain

and Goose – 'don't you touch my grub while I'm away or I'll wallop you black and blue.'

Ma and Kate followed her up the steep, narrow stairs and into a room where three or four people were stretched out on filthy mattresses.

'I can give you a place right by the window,' said Mother Bailey, pushing one of the sleeping bodies out of the way with her boot.

'I'd like to see the view,' said Ma. And, giving Kate a nudge in the ribs and a meaningful look, she went to the window and looked out.

'View?' chuckled the landlady. 'You want a lot for threepence, I must say.'

Kate waited till the woman's back was turned and ran up to the top floor, took a quick look around the empty room where the crossing sweepers slept and hurtled back down again just as her mother was saying, 'Well, I'm not sure.'

She caught Kate's eye. Kate shook her head and mouthed, 'They're not here.'

'Nah. Nah, it doesn't suit,' said Ma.

'Well, I never! Wastin' my time,' grumbled the landlady, stomping back down the stairs. 'Go on, be off with you!'

'I want a word with him first.' Ma pointed at

Captain, who was shovelling something into his mouth behind his landlady's back.

'What d'you want me for?' He stopped eating and wiped his mouth on the back of his hand. 'I haven't done nothin',' he said defensively.

'I want to know what you've done with my boys.'

'What boys?'

'Jem, Ned and Billy.'

'Never heard of them.'

'Oh yeh, you have. I was told you copped them for nickin' a kid's broom.'

'And who are you?' asked Goose.

'I'm their ma.'

The two boys exchanged glances. Many children were kidnapped in London every year. Some were made to work as chimney sweeps, some were forced into the stinking sewers to scavenge for coins or metal, but others suffered a more sinister fate and were never seen again. All too often it was women who searched the streets for these poor wretches, motherly women who lured them with promises of a warm bed and a plentiful supply of food.

'They said their pa's Bert the Beast, the bare-knuckle fighter. That right?' asked Goose.

Ma hesitated. She had seen the look that had

passed between him and Captain, a sly, furtive look that filled her with foreboding.

'What's that got to do with it?' she snapped.

'Is he?' persisted Captain.

'Ma, don't tell them,' Kate whispered urgently in her ear. 'They're up to somethin'.'

'Course it isn't Bert the Beast,' Ma said scornfully. 'Their pa's name's John Smith. And he's never been near a prize ring in his life.'

Again Goose and Captain exchanged glances.

'Nah.' Captain shook his head. 'I've never copped any kids by the name of Smith. You got the wrong party, missus.'

'But—'

'You'd best go,' said Mother Bailey, cutting Ma short. 'You only came here to make trouble. Pretendin' you wanted a room,' she growled. 'Get out and don't come back, d'you hear, or I'll . . . !' She brandished a soup ladle at Ma and Kate menacingly.

'What we goin' to do now, Ma?' said Kate as they hurried away.

'Watch them,' said Ma grimly. 'They know where Jem, Ned and Billy are, no doubt about it. I've never seen such a shifty pair of rogues. We'll hide round that corner –' she indicated an alleyway

142

nearby that led into Great White Lion Street – 'and keep an eye on them.'

'D'you think we should tell Pa?'

'Nah, it's best Pa knows nothin' about it, cos if them sweepers are in league with Killer Kelly—'

'Oh, Ma, you don't think they are, do you?'

'I don't know, my ducky.' Ma sighed, as if the weight of the world was on her shoulders. 'I don't know.'

26

The infants' ward was as bleak as the juveniles'. Thirty or more small children were sitting or lying on the bare floorboards when the orderly arrived with Billy under his arm kicking, scratching and biting.

'Another brat for you,' he said, prying his finger out of Billy's mouth. 'Right little varmint he is too. Where shall I put him, Mrs Chester?' he asked an elderly woman who was sitting on the only chair in the ward, knitting.

'Is there any space left?' she asked, squinting round the room with eyes made milky by cataracts.

'There is now,' said the orderly, kicking two children out of the way. And he dumped Billy on the floor.

'Thank you, Mr Jackson,' she nodded, smiling vaguely in his direction, and went back to her knitting.

Sucking his bleeding finger, in which Billy's

teeth marks could still clearly be seen, the orderly left, locking the door behind him.

Billy looked at the other children. It was impossible to tell which were boys and which were girls, for all were dressed in the same drab clothes and had the same ugly haircrop.

Some were fast asleep, others sat glumly sucking their thumb, scratching, biting their nails, picking their nose or rocking back and forth, back and forth, like mechanical dolls. The two on either side of him sat quite still, gazing vacantly into space as if they were half asleep – or half dead. The only sounds were the constant fusillade of coughs and sneezes and the whimpering of babies who were piled higgledy-piggledy on makeshift mattresses along the walls.

The old woman was totally absorbed in her knitting, frowning and swearing under her breath whenever she dropped a stitch. Stealthily, keeping his eye on her the whole time, Billy stole across the floor on his hands and knees until he reached the door. Then he stood up, grasped the handle and turned it.

Nothing happened.

He pulled harder.

Still nothing happened.

In desperation he started kicking the door and banging on it with his fists.

'It's no use doin' that, lovey,' said the old woman, putting down her knitting. 'Mr Jackson locked it. And I got the other key here,' she said, patting a huge bunch that dangled from a belt at her waist.

Billy burst into tears. 'I want to be with Jem and Ned,' he sobbed.

'Them your brothers?' she said, beckoning him towards her. 'In with the big boys, are they?'

'Yeh.'

'How old are you, lovey?'

Billy held up five fingers.

'Well —' she put a comforting arm around him — 'you'll soon be with them.'

'How soon?'

'About a year.'

'How long's a year?' asked Billy, wiping his tear-stained face and dripping nose on her knitting.

'The other side of Easter.'

'And when's Easter?'

'The other side of Christmas.'

'But Christmas is miles away!'

'Yeh,' the old woman agreed, 'but it'll come. It always does.'

After a while Billy stopped crying and looked around for something to do. But though he tried hard he couldn't persuade any of the children to talk or play with him and there was nothing to look at except dirty walls and even dirtier floors.

'Missus,' Billy said, tugging the old woman's arm and making her drop another stitch, 'what you makin'? Is it a ladder?'

'Nah, it isn't, lovey.' She gave him a toothless smile. 'It's a jacket.'

'Doesn't look much like a jacket to me.'

'That's cos I don't see so well no more, lovey.'

Billy watched her for a while in silence, then he said, 'Missus . . .'

'Now what?'

'I want to go home.'

'You haven't got a home. That's why you're here.'

Billy's eyes filled with tears again and she put down her knitting and pulled his head into her lap while he wept.

'Don't take on so, lovey,' she said, stroking his cheek. 'At least you got a roof over your head and grub to eat – not that it's much,' she grimaced, 'but better than nothin'.'

'But I don't want to stay here,' he wailed.

'You don't have to, lovey, you'll be goin' outside in a minute,' she said, misunderstanding him. 'When you hear the bell you can all go out in the exercise yard.'

'What's exercise?'

'Runnin' and jumpin' – that kind of thing.'

Billy looked up eagerly. 'And can we do handstands and carterwheels?'

'Course you can. You can do whatever you want. Ah, there's the bell now. Come on, lovey, come and enjoy yourself,' said the old woman, unlocking the door and leading the way.

27

Clara was taken to the girls' ward, where she sat on the floor hugging her knees to her chest and staring into space.

As soon as the orderly had gone, five or six girls gathered round her, looking at her quizzically.

'You just come in? I said you just come in?' asked one, but there was not the slightest flicker in Clara's eyes to show that she had even heard her.

'Where you from?' asked another.

'Cat got your tongue?'

'We're sisters,' volunteered the youngest girl. 'I'm Patience and this is Honour, Charity, Hope, Prudence and Faith.' She pointed at the others in turn. 'What's your name?' She squatted on her haunches and peered in Clara's expressionless face. 'We got a brother, he's called Doug, he's in the boys' ward. And our mum and dad are here too – not together, of course,' she continued chattily. 'If we're lucky and there's none of them pesky orderlies around we get to talk to Mum and Dad and Doug sometimes. They tell us what's goin' on. You got anyone in here?'

'I don't think she can hear you proper,' said Hope, the eldest girl. 'She must be deaf.'

'CAN YOU HEAR ME?' Patience bellowed at Clara.

The girl flinched and turned away.

'Yeh, I reckon she can hear all right but she can't talk.'

'Poor thing,' said Hope. 'You can come and sit with us if you like.'

Clara stared straight ahead.

'Please yourself.' Hope shrugged. And she and her sisters wandered away.

28

Unfortunately the yard for the infants had not been designed for exercise or enjoyment. It was as bare as the ward Billy had just escaped from, with brick walls reaching right up to the sky, or so it seemed to the little boy. And the ground was so thickly covered with small pebbles that his heavy boots sank into them and he could barely move, let alone run and jump and do handstands and cartwheels.

Mrs Chester sat herself down on a rickety old chair in one corner and began to doze. Every now and then she would wake up and urge the children to 'Play, loveys, play!' but as they had never learned to play and had nothing to play with anyway they sat on the ground and stared vacantly into space or fell asleep.

Billy gave a deep sigh and for want of anything better to do picked up some pebbles and threw them from one hand to the other in an absent-minded way.

'Want to play fivestones?' he asked the girl sitting next to him, a painfully thin child with sad, red-rimmed eyes and a harelip.

'I said, d'you want to play fivestones?' persisted Billy, nudging her. 'Look, I'll show you. You got to pick them up –' he chose five pebbles of approximately the same size and shape – 'and throw them in the air and catch them on the back of your hand like this. Well –' he pulled a face as the pebbles skittered away – 'you're supposed to. Want to have a try?'

He selected another five pebbles and offered them to her. But she sat very still, her hands folded in her lap, as if she hadn't heard a word he'd said.

'Go on,' Billy urged her.

There was not the slightest acknowledgement from the girl, not even the blink of an eyelid. Thinking that she was off in a dream world or deliberately ignoring him the way his brothers did most of the time, Billy threw a pebble at her to get her attention. Then a second. And a third. They pinged off her shoulders and arms.

Slowly, as if she was waking from a long, deep sleep, she turned and stared at him.

Billy laughed. For the first time he was beginning to enjoy himself. Picking up a handful of pebbles, he tipped them over the girl's head. They slithered down her cheeks and slid off her nose.

She winced and frowned.

Billy got to his feet, picked up more pebbles, looking for the biggest, and dropped them one by one on her head, giggling as they bounced off.

'Don't!' barked the girl.

Billy aimed another pebble, which caught her on the ear.

'I said, DON'T!' She scrambled to her feet and began scooping up handfuls of the stones and hurling them at him.

'Oy!' he cried, putting up his arms to protect himself. 'That's not fair.'

'You started it,' she shouted.

'Yeh, but I was only playin'.'

The other children began to stir then. For a moment they watched in amazement as Billy and the girl pelted each other. Then, cautiously at first, they too began to pick up pebbles and throw them.

Within minutes the yard was full of laughing, screaming children, showering each other and the old woman with stones.

'Lor'!' she cried, pulling her knitting over her head as a large one hit her smack on the nose. 'Are them hailstones?'

At the height of the uproar George Blood appeared, his face scarlet with rage.

'Mrs Chester, what is happenin'? Have these kids gone ravin' mad?' he bellowed, flailing at them with his cane. 'Stop it, you little varmints! Stop it!'

At the sound of Blood's voice all the children fell to the ground and curled up into balls like hedgehogs – all, that is, except Billy. With whoops of delight he continued to dance around the courtyard, shouting at the top of his lungs and flinging pebbles in every direction.

'Boy!' thundered Blood. 'Did you start this?'

'What?'

'I said, DID YOU START THIS?'

The hedgehogs curled up more tightly and began to tremble.

'Nah.' Billy shook his head. 'I just asked her if she wanted to play fivestones –' he pointed at the little girl, who was cowering in terror – 'and then she—'

'*Play*?' The master looked at him in stunned disbelief. 'Have you taken leave of your senses? You're not here to *play*. This is a workhouse. You're here cos you're a pauper, cos your parents are too stupid or too lazy to look after you themselves.'

'Nah, they're not,' protested Billy.

'Silence! How dare you answer me back!' Blood roared. And grabbing Billy by his ears he lifted him off his feet.

'Don't be too hard on him, sir,' pleaded Mrs Chester, as Billy screamed in agony. 'He's only a littl'un.'

'Hold your jaw, old woman. Another word from you and you'll be out of a job.'

'Yes, sir. Sorry, sir,' she mumbled as Billy was dragged away.

29

At midday all the older boys formed a line and with downcast eyes clumped along the corridor and into a room filled with rows and rows of trestle tables. Families were split up, the men sitting separately from their wives, the children away from their parents, and woe betide the anxious father or worried mother who dared cross the divide to speak to their loved ones.

'Can you see Billy?' whispered Jem, looking at the tables where the infants were standing.

'Nah,' Ned whispered back. 'He's not here. He must be feelin' poorly to miss his grub.'

'Poorly? He must be dead.'

At the far end of the room was a large copper cauldron bubbling furiously and on either side of it stood Blood, scowling, and his wife, who had changed for lunch and was now resplendent in a red silk dress and matching bonnet.

Every pauper picked up a bowl, called a porringer,

which Blood half filled with hot water from the cauldron while his wife sprinkled dry oatmeal on the top.

Jem and Ned had never enjoyed a truly delicious meal, like boiled pig's head or jellied cow's tongue or stewed calf's foot, because they were too poor to afford such delicacies, but their mother always gave them a potato or a piece of bread in their soup and, when Pa had managed to steal a chicken or rabbit, a little meat too.

There were no chairs or benches in the room and no knives, forks or spoons on the tables, so that everyone had to stand and eat the meagre meal with their fingers.

'Let us bow our heads and thank God for his goodness in providin' us with this food,' said Blood when all the paupers had taken their places.

Jem looked at the contents of his bowl with suspicion. 'What're them black bits floatin' in it?' he whispered to Doug, who was standing next to him.

'Droppin's.'

'Whose droppin's?'

'Rats' and mice's.'

'No kid?'

'It's true. They taste kind of musty but you get used to them.'

'Not me!'

 157

'Don't be soft, Jem,' Ned hissed at him. 'You got to eat somethin'.'

'And this is all the grub you're goin' to get,' added Doug, tucking into his.

'Grub?' cried Jem indignantly, quite forgetting the rule of silence. 'I wouldn't give this muck to a dog.'

All the paupers stopped slurping gruel and turned to stare at him in disbelief.

'Who spoke?' demanded Blood.

'He did,' said his wife, pointing at Jem with her ladle. 'He's complainin' about the food.'

'Complainin'?' said Blood, loping down the room towards him. 'Is that true, boy?'

'Oh crikey!' breathed Ned. 'Now you're in for it.'

'No, sir, I wasn't complainin', sir,' said Jem. 'All I said was . . . er . . . I said I wouldn't give this much to a dog, sir.'

'So you *were* talkin'?'

'Yeh, I was, sir, but—'

'And you are *still* talkin',' said Blood. And grabbing Jem by the ear he dragged him to the front of the room. 'The punishment for parrots that can't stop squawkin' is five lashes.'

'And another five for complainin' about the food,

Mr Blood,' said his wife. 'I distinctly heard the ungrateful wretch complainin' about the food.'

'That's ten lashes.'

'But all I said was—' protested Jem.

'Fifteen lashes,' said Blood, flexing his cane.

'But—'

'And another five for not callin' you sir, Mr Blood,' said his wife.

'Quite right, Mrs Blood. That's twenty. Take off his bags,' the master barked at two of the orderlies, who pulled Jem's trousers down to his knees and stretched him across a table, gripping his wrists.

Out of the corner of his eye Jem saw Ned starting down the aisle towards him, his eyes blazing, his fists clenched, but Jem frowned and shook his head, warning him to stay away. For a moment Ned paused, his face racked with indecision, then he turned and walked slowly back to his place.

George Blood was no athlete. Given the choice he would have preferred to sit in an armchair with a pipe of rich tobacco in one hand and a tankard of ale in the other. But when, for the good of their souls and the successful running of the workhouse, it became necessary to flog one of the inmates – which happened many times a day – Blood rose to the occasion magnificently.

Grasping his cane firmly in his right hand he took several steps back from the table on which Jem's bottom and thighs lay exposed and, with a little skip and a jump, he brought it swishing down.

'Aargh!' groaned Jem as the cane bit deep into his flesh.

'The boy's a coward, Mr Blood,' sneered his wife. 'He'll be blubbin' in a minute, no doubt.'

But Jem was made of sterner stuff. He gritted his teeth and, though Blood surpassed himself that day, thrashing the boy until his skin was bruised and bleeding and he was nearly faint with pain, Jem never uttered another sound.

'Let that be a lesson to all of you,' said the master, who had worked himself into quite a sweat with so much exercise. 'And you, boy –' he gave Jem another friendly whack on the bottom – 'you can stay there till supper time to think about it.'

30

'Ma,' said Kate, as they hid in the alleyway watching the sweepers' lodging house, 'I know a way to find out where Jem, Ned and Billy are.'

'*What?*' Ma stared at her incredulously. 'Why didn't you say so before, you ninny?'

'Cos I know you wouldn't let me do it.'

'Do what? Oh.' Ma's face fell when she saw where Kate's gaze was resting expectantly. 'Yeh, you're right, Kate, I wouldn't. If Gran was to find out—'

'But she won't, Ma.'

'She will.'

'But she can't do nothin'.'

'Oh yeh, she can. She'll put a nasty spell on you, knowin' her.'

'Paff! Gran's spells never work.'

'They *do* . . . sometimes. Remember when old Mother Perry needled her? Gran put a spell on her and the next day, the very next mornin', all her hair'd fallen out. Her head was as bare as a monkey's bottom. Still is. Face to match, if you ask me,' Ma added tartly.

'Gran couldn't do nothin' to my thatch,' said Kate, running her fingers through her thick ginger curls. 'Oh, come on, Ma, give it me. D'you want to find the boys or not?'

Slowly, reluctantly, with many a dire warning of the terrible disasters that would befall Kate if Gran were to find out, Ma unwrapped her shawl and held out the old woman's crystal ball.

Kate snatched it and crouched down, peering into it intently.

'Can't see nothin',' she said after a while, giving it a jiggle.

'Don't upset it, Kate,' Ma said nervously, backing away.

'I reckon it's not workin'.'

'That's cos it's too bright. You got to do it in the dark.'

'I'm not waitin' that long. Here, give me that.' And pulling the tattered shawl from her mother's shoulders, she draped it over her head and gazed hopefully into the darkened crystal.

'Still can't see nothin'. I reckon it's just an ordinary bit of glass, no different from any other bit of— Oh!'

'What? What?'

'I can see— Oh!'

'The boys? Can you see Jem, Ned and Billy?'

'Nah, I can see Gran. She's sittin' on the steps of our caravan lookin' dumpish. Now she's turnin' her head. Now she's— Oh!'

'Lawks a mercy, girl, stop sayin', "Oh!"' fretted Ma. 'What's Gran doin'?'

'She's lookin' at me.'

'That little hussy's usin' my crystal ball,' fumed Gran. 'I told her, I told everyone, no one looks in that ball except me. She must've gone in my caravan and stole it. She must've—'

'Hold your jaw!' growled Pa, who was lying on his back, gazing despondently into space. 'I don't care who's lookin' at your pesky ball. I don't care if the Queen of England's lookin' at it. If you were any good as a witch—'

'I am not a witch,' interrupted Gran haughtily.

'Well, if you were any good at that magic stuff, you'd know where my boys are.'

Gran fell silent for a moment or two, pulling thoughtfully at the whiskers on her warts. Then she said, 'What day is it, Bert?'

'Monday.'

'And is it a new moon or a full moon?'

'Halfway.'

'Jammy!' The old woman chortled. 'Tonight'll be just right for castin' a spell to find them.'

Pa looked at her askance. 'You reckon you can?' he said doubtfully.

'Course I can. I just need a few things.'

'What kind of things?'

'A hair from the mane of a pure white stallion, the tail feather of a sparrowhawk, the fang of a viper, the claw of a monkey. Oh, and a basin of water.'

'Right,' said Pa, getting to his feet, 'I'll get the basin of water, you get the rest.'

31

'There you go, you pesky little brat,' said Blood, pushing Billy into a small, dark shed between the carpenters' and tinkers' shops in the yard. 'You'll find plenty of mates to play fivestones with in there,' he chortled, slamming the door shut and locking it.

After the bright light Billy could see nothing for a moment or two and he crouched on the floor weeping bitter tears at the harsh treatment he'd suffered at the hands of the workhouse master.

There were no windows in the shed, but a sliver of light streamed through a hole in the roof where a few slates had fallen out or crumbled away and as he adjusted to the gloom the little boy wiped his eyes and looked about him.

'Crimes!' he whispered in horror. 'Oh crimes!' for ranged along one wall were a dozen or more paupers' coffins made of the cheapest wood roughly nailed together and covered by a miserable slip of calico that passed for a shroud.

Renowned for his parsimony in anything relating to the well-being and comfort of the workhouse inmates, Blood had decreed that the mortuary, or dead-house as it was known, should double as a punishment cell for those who had displeased or disobeyed him, and many a child – and men and women too – had shivered the night away in its sombre confines.

Now, Billy was accustomed to death. He saw evidence of it all about him. It was as much a part of his daily life as drunkenness, brutality and crime. Dead dogs, cats, rats and sometimes horses and cows lay rotting where they had fallen in the squalid streets of London's slums. And in an age when poverty and disease claimed people in the prime of life Billy had often seen the body of a dead relative or friend laid out in a coffin. But he had never seen so many coffins at one time and he certainly had never stayed in the same room with them – and on his own.

'When it gets dark,' Jem had informed him during one of his soothing bedtime stories, 'all the stiff'uns come back to life and go lookin' for people so's they can grab their bodies.'

'W-w-why'd they d-do that?' Billy had asked.

'Cos once they get your body they jump in and shove you out so then you're dead and go down to hell 'stead of them. Stiff'uns are always on the look-out for kids, 'specially little kids like you.'

'W-w-why?'

'Cos it means they live longer, you stupe! So don't go nowhere near a coffin after dark, Billy, or . . .' Jem had then given a credible impression of a small boy being consumed by the flames of hell.

Billy crawled into a corner of the dead-house and lay there quaking. It was a bright summer's day but soon, very soon, the sun would disappear and then . . .

'Ma!' cried Billy. 'Ma, don't let them get me. I don't want to die.'

But his mother was far away and there was no one to stand between him and the voracious spirits of the dead.

32

Captain stamped on the floor three times and shouted, 'This extraordinary meetin' of the Trafalgar Square 'n District Crossin' Sweepers' Association is about to begin.'

'"Strordinary" — what does that jawbreaker mean?' asked Ruby.

'Extraordinary,' repeated Captain, who was quite proud that he could pronounce such a long word, 'means it's a special meetin' different from our usual, cos Goose and me got somethin' important to tell you.'

'Like what?'

'If you shut up a minute, Ruby, you'll find out. Goose, give your report, if you please.'

Pulling the same tatty old piece of paper from his pocket as he used for every official pronouncement, Goose began. 'Captain and me were sittin' in the kitchen of this hestablishment this mornin', mindin' our own businesses, when this woman barged in. She had a poppet with her, a very nice piece of goods. A bit older than me, I'd say, but—'

'Get on with it,' Captain urged him.

'So she asked us—'

'*Accused* us, you mean.'

'She accused us of nabbin' Jem, Ned and Billy Parsonski.'

'Who're they?' asked Ruby.

'The three kids that were here last night.'

'Oh, them.'

'She said she was their mother. Only it's a whacker, cos when we asked her if their father was Bert the Beast she said no, their father was a bloke by name of John Smith.'

'And she said he'd never been near a prize ring in his life,' added Captain, stressing every word so that the significance was not lost on the children.

Immediately they all started chattering at once and Captain had to stamp his foot on the floor again and bellow a few colourful threats to bring the meeting to order.

'If you ask me, it's them boys that were tellin' whackers, 'specially the know-all who did all the jabberin',' said Ruby. 'Bert the Beast? Huh!' she scoffed. 'He only said that to make himself important. I'll

wager he's never even seen Bert the Beast, let alone—'

'Yeh, that's what Goose and me thought,' Captain interrupted her, 'but Jack's got somethin' to tell us. Go on, Jack,' he said, turning to a boy smaller than the rest, who seemed overwhelmed by the sudden attention and hung his head, blushing to the roots of his hair.

'Well, go on!' Goose urged him. 'We're not goin' to eat you, you ninny.'

'My uncle follows the Fancy,' began Jack in a voice so faint there were shouts of 'Can't hear nothin'. Speak up! Louder!' 'I said, my uncle follows the Fancy and I asked him about them kids cos I didn't believe them neither . . .' He glanced at Ruby, who nodded vigorously. 'But my uncle said Bert the Beast does have three boys and the oldest – that'd be Jem – is a right shaver, accordin' to my uncle, the kind of rumgumptious gasbag that tells whoppers a mile a minute.'

Another outburst of chattering followed this piece of news.

'So –' Captain shouted the children down again – 'so it's obvious them women are—'

'Snatchers.' Goose finished the sentence for him. 'And we got to find them boys plaguy quick and warn them. Only we got to be careful cos them women're snoopin' on us. Captain and me've seen them. They're hidin' in that alley opposite this very minute watchin' our paddin' ken.'

An uneasy silence fell over the room and the sweepers glanced around nervously as if they too were in imminent danger of being kidnapped.

'Captain!' A girl waved her hand to get his attention. 'Why don't you ask Clara where them boys are. She was with them last.'

'Yeh, good idea. Clara! Clara!'

'She isn't here, Captain,' said Tilly.

'And she wasn't at her pitch today neither,' said Danny.

'But Clara's always at her pitch.'

'She's never away.'

'You don't think . . .?'

'She's been snatched as well?'

'Oh crimes, not Clara.'

Pandemonium broke out again and it took a few minutes before Captain could make himself heard.

'Now listen,' he bellowed, 'we got to find Clara and Jem and Ned and Billy. We'll get out the usual way tonight, after dark, so's them women don't see us.'

33

Jem was made to stand in a corner of the dinner ward for the rest of the day. All through supper he watched hungrily as the other boys wolfed down their food – all, that is, except Ned. Jem could see his brother standing next to Doug, his face pale and drawn, the bowl of gruel in his hand untouched.

'You goin' to eat that or not?' demanded Blood, jabbing a finger at it.

Ned mumbled something.

'SPEAK UP!'

'I said, nah, sir, I'm not, sir.'

'Not good enough for you, eh?' Blood goaded him.

'Yeh, it is, sir. But I'm not hungry, sir.'

'Not hungry?' Blood chuckled. 'We must be feedin' you too much. Remember to give this boy half rations in the future, dearest,' he shouted to his wife. 'And it seems a pity to waste that,' he said, snatching the bowl and sloshing the hot gruel in

Ned's face. 'There,' he beamed, 'now you've had a nice wash. You look a lot better.'

Despite the searing pain in his bottom and thighs Jem made to help his brother, but Ned met his eye and frowned.

When supper was over Blood and three of the orderlies frogmarched Jem to the boys' bed ward, a large, dismal room as bare as the day ward except for piles of straw scattered haphazardly over the floor and covered with strips of filthy cloth that might have started out their life as sheets.

An overpowering stench arose from two overflowing buckets in the centre in which the boys relieved themselves.

'Right, that's your bed,' said Blood, throwing Jem on to one of the piles. 'We've given you the best,' he added with a smile, 'right under a hole in the roof and next to a thunderin' great crack in the wall, so you'll be nice and cool in this hot weather. But' – the smile quickly turned to a sneer – 'come the winter you'll get soaked when it rains and you'll freeze to death when the wind blows. That's if you live that long. That'll learn you to keep your mouth shut.'

'You all right, Jem?' whispered Ned, leaning over him anxiously when Blood had gone.

'Course I am,' grunted Jem, trying not to wince, for the hard straw pierced his torn skin unmercifully. 'But I'm goin' to kip on the floor,' he said, easing himself off the straw with clenched teeth. 'I reckon it'll be a mite more comfortable.'

Doug stole across the room, stooping low when he passed the door in case one of the orderlies was spying on them through the keyhole, and knelt down by Jem.

'You were a stupe gettin' on the wrong side of Blood like that,' he whispered. 'He's got it in for you now.'

'I'm goin' to kill him,' growled Jem.

'Oh yeh? You and who else?'

'I don't need no help.'

'Don't be soft. Dozens of people've tried to rub him out, but he's strong, built like a bull elephant with a temper to match. Besides, he's always got a load of orderlies hangin' around him. Bruisers!' He spat the word. 'They'd finish you off before you got anywhere near Blood.'

'Soon as I get out of here I'm goin' to tell everyone about him. I'm goin' to—'

'Nah, won't do no good.' Doug shook his head. 'He's safe, is Blood. He's like that with the Board of

Guardians.' He crossed his middle finger over the index finger and waved them under Jem's nose.

'Who's the Guardians?'

'Load of old fogeys who run this place. They come round now and then –' Doug got to his feet and walked up and down, his belly pushed out, sticking his thumbs in his pockets and looking down his nose like a pompous old man – 'take a quick look around –' he put an imaginary monocle in his eye and squinted at the ward – 'tell Blood what a good job he's doin'. Thank him for savin' them so much money – by not givin' us nothin' to eat,' he added wryly. 'Then they go up to Blood's rooms and have a splendacious dinner. Nah, you'd be wastin' your time complainin' to them or the crushers. They don't care about us. Nobody does.'

34

As the sun sank slowly behind the grim walls of the workhouse fear rose in Billy's throat until it threatened to choke him. The carpenters, who had spent the whole day banging and cutting, laid down their hammers and saws, the tinkers put aside the kettles and saucepans they had been mending, and yawning and stretching their aching limbs they trudged away to snatch a few hours' sleep before it was time for the crushing grind of their daily work to begin once more.

A stillness settled over the yard, broken only by the intermittent groans of a sick woman in the fever-and-foul-cases ward which, conveniently, was opposite the dead-house.

The moon nudged the sun out of the sky and a sliver of its silvery light filtered through the hole in the dead-house roof, casting an eerie glow over the coffins. Billy squeezed himself into a tight ball in the darkest corner, hoping against hope that the spirits of the dead would overlook him in their search for available bodies.

A couple of tomcats who had taken a violent dislike to each other and spent the last half-hour or more growling and hissing suddenly flew at each other's throats with a screech and Billy, startled, cried out. He slapped a hand over his mouth but it was too late. Someone or something had heard him. There was a movement beneath the shroud of the coffin closest to him, a scrabbling, groping movement, the kind a hand makes when it's searching for a way out.

Billy stared at the shroud, transfixed. He could neither blink, swallow nor breathe. His very blood seemed to have stopped coursing round his body. Deep inside him a voice clamoured, 'Scream! Scream for help!' but his mouth wouldn't open and no sound would have emerged even if it had.

At length the shroud was pushed aside and something appeared. A hand? A black, hairy hand? Billy's eyes opened so wide they nearly fell out of his head. Hadn't Jem told him time and time again the devil was covered in thick black hair from the tip of his horns to the toes of his cloven feet?

The 'something' peeked over the edge of the

coffin, its beady eyes surveying Billy intently for a moment. Then it jumped on to the floor and scuttled away on its four paws, squeaking loudly.

35

There were three exits from the crossing sweepers' lodgings: the front door (if there had been one), the back door (similar problem) and what Captain had called 'the usual way'.

One of the merits of the Victorian house was the cellar, and the residents of Great White Lion Street, being of a sociable disposition, had knocked holes in the walls of their cellars big enough for their neighbours to crawl through should they get a sudden urge to pay them a visit – usually in the middle of the night. So, if on glancing out of his window the gentleman who lived in the house at the bottom of Great White Lion Street saw two constables on his doorstep who wanted to have a word with him about the removal of certain valuable items from a mansion in Regent's Park, he put on his cap, bid his wife and children farewell and ran through the cellars, emerging from the back door of the house at the top of the street.

In order to avoid Ma Perkinski's watchful eye, Captain, Goose and the crossing sweepers followed the same route that night, nodding at the old couple who lived in the top house as they sat at their kitchen table slurping pease pudding.

'Now listen,' Captain whispered as the children gathered round him in the couple's dingy back yard. 'See if you can find out where Clara and them boys are, but be careful. Don't get people suspicious. If they ask you why you want to know, say them kids owe you money.'

'How long we got, Captain?' said Goose.

'Be back here by midnight.'

36

Gran trudged into the yard behind the brickworks just before the church bell tolled midnight.

'Well?' said Pa impatiently as the old woman sank on to the steps of the caravan with a weary sigh.

'I've walked my trotters to bits, Bert,' she moaned, pulling off her boots and rubbing her aching feet.

'Never mind that. Did you get the stuff for the spell?'

'I got a hair from the mane of a horse, but it wasn't a stallion and it wasn't white. Matter of fact, it was a mare and she was grey and got quite shirty about it too. Gave me a right wallop on the drumstick.' Gran lifted her skirts to show Pa a colourful bruise on her leg. 'Then I tried to pull a claw out of the organ grinder's monkey, but it bit me —' she held out her arm to show the little creature's teeth marks — 'so I took one off a dead cat. And the snake swallower said his viper didn't have no fangs and anyway it was a grass snake, but it was sheddin' its skin so he gave me a bit.' Gran threw a few dry scales on the ground.

'What about the hawk's feather?'

Gran heaved another sigh. 'London's full of birds – sparrows, starlin's, blackbirds, robins – but no hawks, leastwise none I could see. So I got this instead.' She held up a feather.

Pa peered at it. 'That's a pigeon's,' he said.

'I know, I know. Best I could do, Bert. And the pesky varmint gave me a nasty peck.'

'Nah, I don't want to see it,' said Pa hastily as Gran started to hoick up her skirts again. 'Will the spell work with all this mullock?'

'We'll give it a try, Bert. Go and get the water. Oh, and some grub too.'

'But we've only got a bit left and we've got to keep that for breakfast.'

'We've got to offer it to the spirits, as a thank you for helpin' us, Bert. Nah, don't get snaggy,' she said as Pa began to huff and puff, 'they won't scorf it, they never do.'

Pa went into the caravan and came out carrying a rusty basin full of water, the end of a dry loaf, two cold potatoes and a few limp cabbage leaves which he put on the ground in front of Gran.

'You sit one side and I'll sit the other,' she said. 'And don't say nothin', Bert, nothin' at all. Spirits can't stand chatterbaskets.' And picking up the hair of the old grey mare she waved it over the basin three times and dropped it in, intoning, '*Les see kedo, les see kedo, les see kedo,*' in a sepulchral voice.

'Let's see who?' whispered Pa.

'Stow it, Bert!' Gran admonished him.

Picking up the pigeon's feather she waved it too over the basin three times before dropping it in, repeating, '*Les see kedo, les see kedo, les see kedo.*'

'But who's Kedo?' hissed Pa.

'Hold your jaw!'

'But I don't want to see Kedo, you daft old hay-bag. I want to see Jem, Ned and—'

'It's a Romany spell, Bert. I'm talkin' in Romany,' Gran snapped. 'I thought you'd know that, seein' as how we're gypsies.'

'Oh . . . oh, right. Yeh . . . yeh, of course it's Romany. I know that. It's just that I . . . er . . . I've forgotten for the moment what "*les see kedo*" means.'

'I'll tell you later,' said Gran, who had also forgotten – if she ever knew. And picking up the cat's claw and the snake's scales she dropped them in the water.

'Oh drat!' she muttered.

'Now what?'

'I can't do the spell without my magic wand.'

'Where is it?'

'In my caravan, of course, back at Devil's Acre. I should have brought it with me. I should have brought all my magic potions too, but you made me leave so fast I—'

'All right, all right, don't start that again,' Pa cut her short. 'Can't we use somethin' else for a wand? What about the old wooden spoon Ma uses for stirrin' gruel?'

'It'll have to do. And hurry up! The moon'll be shrinkin' in a minute and the spell won't work.'

'I'm lookin', I'm lookin',' Pa shouted from inside the caravan, 'but I can't find the pesky thing. I don't know where Liza keeps it. Come and help me.'

'Lawks a mercy!' exclaimed Gran, hauling herself to her feet. 'Have I got to do everythin'?' And muttering about how useless men were, especially when it came to finding things, she staggered up the steps of the caravan.

It took a while to rummage through the pile of

rags and rubbish that Ma kept 'in case we ever need them', but at last the wooden spoon was found.

'Come on plaguy quick, Bert,' said Gran, 'or we'll be too late.'

But they were already too late.

The pig, enticed by the sight and smell of food, had broken down the flimsy wall of his lean-to shed, devoured the bread, potato and cabbage leaves and washed them down with the water.

'Blimey!' cried Gran when she saw the empty basin. 'All that work for nothin'.'

37

All the sweepers were back in the lodging house by midnight, most of them looking downcast, for although they had combed the streets far and wide and asked everyone they knew, none had managed to track down Jem, Ned and Billy. None that is except Captain.

'I got a important bit of news,' he said, looking well pleased with himself.

'*I* got a important bit of news, you mean,' Ruby interrupted him.

'I found out that—'

'*I* found it out.'

'All right,' Captain conceded sulkily, 'you found it out.'

'Found out what?' said Goose. 'Lor's sake, get on with it.'

'Like I was about to say,' continued Ruby, with a disdainful glance at Captain, 'after we all split up I went up St Giles to see some kids I know, but they hadn't seen Clara nor them boys and not heard nothin' about them neither, but as I was comin' back I bumped into Constable Ross and—'

'Oh crikey!' exclaimed Goose.

'And I asked him—'

'You did *what*?'

'You *talked* to a *crusher*?'

'Yeh, I did.' Ruby thrust her chin out. 'I like him.'

This was greeted with stares of disbelief.

'What did she say? What did she say?' asked the ones at the back who hadn't heard.

'Said she likes crushers.'

'Nah! Really? Must be off her chump.'

'Ravin' barmy.'

'Should be locked up.'

'I didn't say I like *all* crushers,' insisted Ruby. 'I'm not that looney tic. But I like Constable Ross. He's all right – well, for a policeman. And he said he knows where Clara is. Them boys too. He said they were picked up by a crusher, a cove called Murray, a mate of his who—'

'Get on with it, Ruby,' said Captain impatiently, 'else we'll be here all night. Where are them kids?'

'In the workhouse. Flogger Flynn sent them there.'

 187

'The workhouse?' exclaimed the others in horror, for the workhouse was more frightening to them than prison or a lunatic asylum. 'Which one?'

'The Strand.'

'Lor',' gasped Goose in a hoarse whisper. 'George Blood's the master there.'

'We got to get them out,' said Captain, 'plaguy quick.'

'Yeh, but how?'

'I know.' A hand shot up at the back of the room.

'What, Fred?' said Captain eagerly.

'Clara's mum can get her out. All she has to do is go to the house and tell old Blood she wants her kid back and he can't stop her. Same with them boys.'

'Jammy!' exclaimed the sweepers.

'Nah.' Captain shook his head. 'It's all right for Clara, but them boys don't have no mum nor dad.'

'Course they do. Their dad's Bert the Beast.'

'Yeh, but I heard nobody's seen him since the big fight with Killer Kelly. They reckon he and his missus must've scarpered.'

At that all the sweepers fell into a glum silence. They were used to people abandoning their children because they didn't want them or, more often, couldn't afford to look after them, but Goose's words had brought back sad memories of their own parents, many of whom had also 'scarpered', never to be seen again.

'We got to get Jem, Ned and Billy out of the Strand Workhouse before them women find out they're there,' said Goose, 'or else they'll go along, pretend them boys are their kids and get them out and . . .'

'Nah, they won't,' said Ruby. 'Why should they? There are plenty of other kids on the street to snatch.'

'Yeh, but for some reason them women want Jem, Ned and Billy . . . They do!' he insisted as Ruby started to protest again. 'Else why did they come here and ask me and Captain about them?'

'Goose is right.' Captain nodded. 'They're after them Parsonski kids – so we've got to put them off the scent.'

'Why?' said Ruby.

'What d'you mean "why"?'

'Why've we got to waste our time savin' them pesky kids?'

'Cos we all swore an oath, includin' you, that we'd help them if they got in trouble just like they'd help us – that's why,' said Captain angrily. 'We're all brothers now.'

'And sisters,' snapped Ruby.

'Yeh, all right, we're all brothers and sisters, so we got to look out for each other.'

'How we goin' to put them two women off the scent, Captain?' said Goose.

'You lot're goin' to go out in the mornin' and act suspicious like, pretend you know where the boys are, and they'll follow you.'

'But where'll we go?'

'Anywhere, long as it's nowhere near the Strand Workhouse. Go the other direction.'

'And what about you?'

'I'll go to the Workhouse, of course, and get them kids out.'

'What, just like that?' scoffed Ruby.

'Yeh, just like that,' retorted Captain. 'Anyone want to come with me?'

A forest of hands shot up.

'And how exactly are you goin' to get in there?' demanded Ruby. 'It's got walls higher than a mountain and a porter on the gate that'd knock your teeth out if you tried to get past him – not to mention Blood and his cronies.'

'Ah . . .' Captain tapped the side of his nose and gave a sly smile. 'I know a way in, a secret way.'

'Oh yeh, and what's that?'

'Through the sewers.'

Immediately all the hands went down.

'Lawks,' muttered someone, 'you're on your own.'

'Lanky'll come with me, won't you?' Captain said to a boy taller than the others with blond hair and grey, doleful eyes.

'Nah,' said Lanky without hesitation. 'Nah, I'm not goin' down no sewers, not for no one.'

'Don't then –' Captain shrugged – 'only you can't belong to the Association no more, cos we don't want lily-livered coves like you, do we?' He turned to the other sweepers.

'Nah, we don't,' they cried enthusiastically, relieved that Captain hadn't chosen one of them.

Lanky hesitated, but only for a moment. He had never known his parents, the grandmother who had cared for him had died when he was four and for a year or more he had wandered the streets, frightened, hungry and alone until the crossing sweepers had taken him in. They were his family, his friends. And the room he shared with them was his home.

'I was only kiddin',' he said, doing his best to grin. 'Course I'll come with you, Captain.'

38

Jem hardly slept that night. His bottom hurt, the heat was stifling, the floor hard, the straw crawling with bedbugs, lice, ticks and fleas, spiders ran over his face, mice skittered up and down his legs and rats nibbled tentatively at his toes.

But it was the ceaseless cacophony of the workhouse that kept him awake, the sound of windows being smashed and doors violently kicked, the shouting and swearing from the tramps and beggars' ward as they set about each other with heads, knuckles and feet, the gibbering and fitful laughter from the ward where the lunatics and mentally ill lay, some in straitjackets, others tied to posts, the piercing wail of frightened, hungry children in the infants' ward and the barrage of snores, farts, coughs, sneezes, snuffles and sighs from the restless boys in his own.

*

Clara too lay awake most of the night, her eyes wide open, her mind in turmoil. If only . . . The wretched words whirled around her head, tormenting her with their futility. If only she hadn't left little Pip with a stranger, if only she hadn't tripped over the cat, if only Constable Ross hadn't found her . . .

Where was Pip now? Would they ever see him again? Her mother . . . Clara groaned as if in pain. Her mother would never forgive her for leaving him with that woman.

She sat up, trying to shake the torturous thoughts out of her head. At the far end of the ward she could see Doug's sisters, all of them fast asleep, their arms around each other despite the heat, a look approaching contentment on their faces. They had each other. They had a mother and father, albeit in another ward. They had a brother.

Clara sighed. She had no one. With Pip gone and her mother—

'You all right?' asked the girl lying next to her in a sleepy voice.

Clara stared into her lap. She had tried to speak many times, but there seemed to be a lump in her throat so big, so heavy, it almost choked her and she couldn't get the words past it.

'Huh! Hoity toity!' huffed the girl, misunderstanding Clara's silence. 'I don't want to talk to you neither.'

And she turned her back on her.

Just before dawn an orderly came for Clara and took her to Blood's apartments. The master was already up and dressed and in his usual surly mood. In trying to shave some of the thick black bristles off his cheeks he had cut himself badly and blood had trickled down his neck in crimson rivulets, drying in an ugly crust.

'Now listen,' he said, 'I want this parlour swept and the fire cleaned and the furniture polished and every one of them bits and pieces –' he indicated the mass of ornaments with a sweep of the hand – 'every one, mind, dusted. And when you done in here you'll do the dinin' room. And I want that done proper too. If I see so much as a speck of dust or anythin' broken, even if it's the tiniest chip, you know what'll happen to you, don't you?' He rubbed his hands together, clearly relishing the prospect. 'I said, DON'T YOU?'

Clara looked him straight in the eye but made not the slightest movement.

He went to strike her but something about the

girl, a stillness he had seldom if ever encountered in a workhouse child, stayed his hand.

'And another thing —' he dropped his voice to a whisper — 'don't make no noise. Mrs Blood likes to sleep late and she gets very kicksy if she's woke up. D'you hear what I'm sayin'? Oh, get out of my way!' he snarled, pushing Clara aside.

And he left the room.

Clara was no stranger to living on the streets of London. When they could, her family rented space in a lodging house, but when times were hard they risked arrest by sleeping on the street — the pavement was their home, the gutter their chair, a shop doorway their bed.

It was hardly surprising, therefore, that the girl was nonplussed when faced with the task of cleaning the Bloods' parlour. Nevertheless she set to work, flicking her duster over the myriad ornaments in a desultory way, pausing now and then to look more closely at an ornate clock or a bowl of wax cherries or a stuffed animal, its beady eyes so lifelike, so piercing, that she flinched and backed away.

A porcelain figure caught her eye, a Dresden shepherdess of simpering prettiness, but in reaching out to touch it her sleeve brushed against a crystal goblet, sending it crashing into the grate where it shattered into smithereens.

Alarmed that she might have woken Mrs Blood, Clara uttered a cry, which came out somewhere between a gasp and a strangulated squeal. To her surprise there came an answering cry, 'Preeh, preeh', from a wickerwork cage by the window.

The girl hastily swept up the shards of glass, tipped them into a vase and rearranged the stand so that the loss of the goblet would not be noticed. Then, clasping her hands above her head to keep them out of harm's way, she squeezed between tables, chairs, sofas and footstools until she reached the cage and pulled off the embroidered cloth that covered it to reveal a skylark. Startled by the sudden movement, the bird began to fly back and forth in a frenzy.

Clara bent down and peered at it. She had never given any thought to birds before, never realized how beautiful they were, with their delicate bodies, tiny feet and iridescent wings. They were just there, all around her, pecking crumbs from the pavement or perching on a wall or flying over rooftops.

The skylark settled down after a while and Clara watched, entranced, as it began to preen itself, dressing its white waistcoat assiduously with its sharp little bill, pausing once in a while to look up at her with inquisitive eyes.

A shaft of sunlight penetrated the Stygian gloom of the parlour and fell full upon the cage. Immediately the skylark stopped preening and began to throw up its head in an agitated way, as if the sunshine reminded it there was a beautiful world outside.

Clara felt a surge of emotion sweep through her, pity for the tiny creature and fury at the Bloods for condemning it so unfairly to life imprisonment in its miserable little cell.

She glanced at the sash window. All she had to do was lift it a few inches and open the cage. She would be viciously punished, but she didn't care. Only the bird mattered, setting it free, watching it fly far, far away from the workhouse and all its horrors . . .

Her hand moved towards the cage but at that moment the door burst open and the master came in, his mouth set in a grim line.

Clara sprang to her feet, but he seemed not to notice her. Crossing quickly to the bedroom he knocked on the door and upon hearing an imperious 'Come!' he went in, saying, 'I'm so sorry to disturb you, dearest,' in the obsequious voice he used with his wife.

Clara never heard why he had dared to intrude upon his wife's slumbers at such an ungodly hour for he shut the door behind him. But whatever his reason it clearly irritated Mrs Blood, for her voice rose from a waking grunt to a strident bark.

Moments later the master came out, looking like a whipped dog, growled, 'Go and help your mistress, girl,' at Clara, and strode away.

39

Jem was just drifting off to sleep at five o'clock when the rising bell jarred him awake. The deep cuts on his bottom were so agonizing he could hardly move and he lay for a few moments, gathering the strength to get up.

'You all right?' asked Ned.

'Yeh, course I am, except I didn't get much shut-eye, what with the racket goin' on all night.'

'Me neither.' Ned grimaced. 'The kid next to me kept spittin' down my neck when he coughed and every time someone peed in the slop bucket it spilled over and drenched my feet. And I wish we could wear our own gear, especially our boots. These ones are so tight,' he complained, struggling to pull them on, 'I got blisters big as balloons and . . . Watch out!' His voice dropped. 'Blood's comin'.'

Jem struggled to his feet, doing his utmost not to cry out as the cuts on his bottom opened up and began to bleed again.

 199

'Everyone outside,' shouted Blood. 'And you, boy –' he pointed at Jem – 'you empty the slop buckets.'

'Where, sir?'

'Where, sir? Where, sir?' Blood mocked him. 'Down the drain in the yard, of course, you numbskull.'

Staggering under the weight, Jem carried the heavy buckets into the yard, emptied them down the drain and took his place in the long line of boys waiting to wash their hands under a tap.

Breakfast was scarcely more nourishing than supper – a few slimy cabbage leaves floating in hot water.

'Now listen,' said Blood when the miserable meal was over, 'I just got word that the Guardians're comin' today. They're comin' to inspect the workhouse. You know what that means, don't you?'

'Yeh, sir,' mumbled the paupers in unison.

'Good. Now I want you all to be on your best behaviours.' The master walked slowly up and down the lines, slapping his cane against his thigh ominously. 'If they ask you a question, you answer them honest, you understand? Just tell them you're comfortable. Not too comfortable, mind,' he cautioned. 'I don't want them thinkin' you're enjoyin' yourselves at their expense. Same goes for the food. You tell them it's satisfactory. Just satisfactory, nothin' more. And if I hear one word of complaint out of anyone –' he stopped in front of Jem, glaring at him – 'their life won't be worth livin'. Got that?' He pushed his hairy face into Jem's. 'I said, GOT THAT?'

'Got it,' said Jem, looking him straight in the eye, 'sir.'

40

It was fortunate for Ma and Kate that it was summertime. Had it been damp, foggy November or piercingly cold January they would have had a hard time of it, but with the temperature well into the eighties, even at night, they were more comfortable in the open air than in their stuffy caravan – especially with Pa and Gran snoring loud enough to lift the roof off.

'We'll take it in turns to sleep,' said Ma. 'You keep watch first, Kate, and keep a sharp eye out for crushers, cos if they find us they'll nail us for vagrancy. And watch out for anyone lurkin' around lookin' suspicious.'

'W-what d'you mean, "suspicious", Ma?' said Kate nervously.

'Ugly customers that look like they're goin' to slit our throats or nick our boots.'

'So what'll I do?'

'Wake me up, of course.'

Ma had barely stretched out on the pavement with her head resting comfortably on a doorstep when Kate hissed in her ear, 'Ma! Ma! Wake up!'

'Why? What's wrong?' said Ma, leaping to her feet, her heart racing.

'That cove over there —' Kate nodded at a boy about her own age standing on the other side of the street – 'he's starin' at me.'

'Oy, you, who you lookin' at?' Ma yelled at him.

'Her.' The boy pointed to Kate. 'I've just given my girl the boot cos she's a right trollop. But I like the look of her. She's a nice piece of goods, she is.' He gave Kate a cheeky grin. 'Want to come home with me, my poppet?'

'Nah, she does not, you little varmint!' said Ma. 'And if you don't hook it plaguy quick the only thing you'll take home is a backside tanned black and blue.'

'All right, all right, no need to get crusty,' complained the boy, thrusting his hands in his pockets and slouching away.

As soon as he had turned the corner Ma settled down to sleep again, but no sooner had she closed her eyes than Kate shook her shoulder roughly.

'Look! Look!' The girl pointed with a trembling hand at a figure walking towards them. 'Look at its head, Ma, it's huge and . . . Oh crimes, look at its face . . . Aargh!' she cried, hiding behind her mother.

Ma took one look at the figure with its spiky horsehair wig, white-painted face and huge red-nose and snapped, 'Don't be such a stupe, Kate, it's a clown. You've seen plenty of them on the street. Had a good day, love?'

'Diabolical,' muttered the clown, his huge horseshoe mouth drooping even more. 'Nobody's comin' out in this hot weather, leastwise not the folk with money. I've been playin' the fool since eight o'clock this mornin' – jumpin' and tumblin' and turnin' somersaults and singin' and dancin' and tellin' jokes. And for what?' He held out his hand to show Ma the few coins he had collected. 'They won't buy a night's lodgin' and vittals for me and the wife and kids, will they? I tell you, it's no fun bein' a clown, no fun.' And with a deep sigh he walked on, a pathetic, grotesque figure in his red and black polka-dot outfit with its full sleeves and frills and neck ruff.

'Right, now I'm goin' to *try* to get a bit of sleep, Kate,' said her mother pointedly.

'Nah, that's not fair, Ma.' Kate pouted. 'It's my turn.'

'*Your* turn? *Your* turn? I like that, I really do! Every time I close my eyes . . .'

Kate, who had been leaning against the wall, slid down it and came to rest on her haunches, her head on her knees. 'I'm right done up, Ma,' she said, yawning.

'Go to sleep then, my pet,' said Ma, softening.

'Wake me when it's my turn,' mumbled Kate.

'Course I will,' said Ma. And there she stood all night, looking up and down the street, mindful of every movement, every sound, while her daughter lay sleeping as peacefully as a kitten.

Well before dawn the streets of Seven Dials came to life. Doors opened and people set off for work, legal or otherwise. The men went to factories, building sites, markets – anywhere muscles were needed. The women trundled handcarts piled high with washing and ironing back and forth to their customers or hurried to sweatshops where they slaved for ten hours a day or more with barely a break, making men's shirts for a penny a piece. One or two of the children went to a Ragged School, where they learned the rudiments of reading, writing and arithmetic, but most went to Regent Street or some other busy thoroughfare to earn, beg or steal money as best they could.

'Anythin' happenin', Ma?' asked Kate, yawning herself awake. 'Them crossin' sweepers up yet?'

'Nah. No one's come out of that house all night.'

'I could do with somethin' to eat. Got any money?'

Ma reached into her cleavage and pulled out two pennies. 'Go and get a bit of bread and a penn'orth of cheese,' she said. 'Oh, and Kate,' she called after the girl as she hurried away, 'don't scorf the lot before you get back.'

'Lor', Ma.' Kate bridled at the suggestion. 'I'm not like Billy!'

Some time later, when Ma and Kate had eaten their frugal breakfast, Goose poked his head round the doorway of the lodging house and looked furtively up and down the street.

'He looks fishy,' whispered Kate, peering around her mother's shoulder.

'He's up to somethin' all right,' agreed Ma.

The boy stepped into the street, hunching his shoulders as if to make himself smaller, if not invisible, and checking once again that the coast was clear he beckoned to the other sweepers to follow him. One by one they crept out, their eyes darting everywhere, and huddling tightly together they hurried down the street like smugglers in the night.

'I reckon we should keep an eye on that lot,' said Ma. 'I'll follow them.'

'But, Ma –' Kate caught her shoulder and pulled her back – 'you're not goin' to leave me here all on my own, are you?'

'You stay here and keep an eye on Captain. When he comes out, follow him.'

'But, Ma—'

'Lor', Kate, don't be so lily-livered', said Ma angrily, shaking her off.

'There goes one,' said Captain, watching Ma from an upstairs window as she stole down the street, staring into shop windows or diving into doorways whenever Goose or one of the sweepers glanced over their shoulder.

'Not much good at it, is she?' sniggered Lanky.

The two boys watched Ma until she was out of sight. Then, 'Right,' chortled Captain, well pleased with his ruse, 'she's gone. Let's get goin'.'

'But what about the girl?'

'By the time she realizes she's been watchin' this place all day for nothin', it'll be too late. Come on!'

The two boys hurtled down the stairs, nearly

 207

bowling over their landlady, who was on her way up.

'And where do you think you're off to in such a hurry?' she asked, squinting at them suspiciously. 'You nicked somethin' off me, have you?'

'You got nothin' worth nickin', Mother Bailey,' said Captain, giving her a saucy wink, 'apart from a couple of loose floorboards. And we wouldn't get a farthin' for them.'

'We're goin' to the Strand Workhouse,' explained Lanky.

'Oh really? My paddin' ken's not good enough for you then? You're lookin' for handsomer accommodations, are you?' she said, laughing hugely.

'We're goin' to rescue some kids.'

'Out of the Workhouse?' she scoffed. 'Never!'

41

George Blood was used to the occasional visit from the Board of Workhouse Guardians, a dozen or so local businessmen and tradesmen, almost all of whom had taken the job in order to make useful business and social contacts rather than to improve the lot of the poor and sick, in whom they had no interest whatsoever. But he was surprised and angry that they had given him such short notice. Although the whole purpose of such visits was to catch the master unawares, the Guardians of the Strand Union normally gave Blood at least a week to clean the place and evict the more unruly inmates.

He was even more surprised when the porter hurried up to him that hot morning and said, 'Some people to see you, master. Not the usual lot that come round. These are real toffs. I left them in the yard. D'you want me to take them up to your rooms?'

Blood shook his head. He was in no mood to entertain a group of strangers, aristocratic or not. Muttering under his breath, he lumbered down the stairs and into the courtyard, where a group of elegantly dressed men and women stood waiting.

'Mr Blood?' said one, raising his top hat and giving the master a courteous nod. 'I am Sir Edmund Eden.' He stepped forward with outstretched hand. 'And this —' he indicated the lady standing next to him — 'is Miss Lucinda Twine. I am the chairman and Miss Twine is the secretary of the Workhouse Visiting Society.'

'Never heard of it,' said Blood, taking the man's hand with extreme reluctance.

'It was established to look into the administration of workhouses and the well-being of the inmates.'

'Well, you'll find nothin' amiss here,' retorted Blood. 'I run a tight ship. There's no waste. But,' he added quickly, 'everyone gets their fair share. Nobody never complains. They got no reason to.'

'I'm sure they haven't, master,' said Sir Edmund with a smile. 'Now, sir, would you do us the courtesy of showing us around?'

'I can't. I don't have time. I got the Guardians

comin' this mornin', the *proper* guardians,' Blood added with an insolent grin.

Miss Twine frowned. 'You *know* they're coming, master? They have warned you of their arrival? I thought that was strictly against the spirit if not the letter of the law.'

Too late Blood realized his insolent tongue had dug a dangerous hole into which he was about to step.

Hastily he retreated. 'Nah, they didn't tell me. Course they didn't. I was just . . . er . . . just tipped off by someone, a mate of mine who works for one of them. He said they might be comin'—'

'I imagine your informant was referring to us.' Sir Edmund cut him short. 'Now, sir, would you do us the courtesy of—'

'Yeh, yeh, all right,' Blood said grudgingly. 'What d'you want to see?'

'Everything.'

It was clear from their faces that most of the members of the Workhouse Visiting Society had never been in a workhouse before. And though every person they spoke to said they were 'Comfortable, thank you, sir' and the food was 'Satisfactory, thank you, madam', they became increasingly dismayed.

'Poor little things,' they sighed, when they saw the rows and rows of babies in the infants' ward.

'How do you keep them so quiet?' enquired Miss Twine.

'I give them gin and peppermint, ma'am,' said Mrs Chester, gazing up at her with sightless eyes. 'And if that doesn't work I give them a dose of laudanum. That dulls their little brains so's they don't cry.'

'Laudanum?' gasped one of the women. 'But that's a powerful drug. It's—'

'Opium,' said another. 'A terrible thing to give an innocent child.' And they all glared at Mrs Chester.

'It is not her fault,' Miss Twine admonished them in a whispered aside. 'She is only doing what she has been told to –' she gave Blood a baleful look – 'by people who ought to know better.'

In horrified silence they followed Blood into wards where lunatics banged and screeched, where the crippled, the deaf and the blind lay on the floor sighing and groaning, where the old huddled together in misery.

'Are there no able-bodied men and women in this workhouse?' asked Sir Edmund.

'Course there are. We put them to work. The

women work in the laundry or kitchen and the men –' Blood hesitated – 'do other things.'

'What other things?'

'Oh.' Blood shuffled uneasily. 'This and that.'

'I should like to see them doing "this and that",' insisted Sir Edmund. 'Now.'

Muttering under his breath about people wasting his precious time, Blood led them down the stairs and across the courtyard to a corrugated-iron shed. The small windows were barred, but through the panes of broken glass they could see a number of men pounding blocks of stone with heavy bars of iron.

'They got to break them small enough so's the pieces go through that,' Blood explained, pointing to a large sieve on the floor.

'Poor souls,' murmured Miss Twine, watching the men as they smashed and sifted the blocks of stone till their arms ached and their hands blistered.

'I don't see what's poor about them,' retorted Blood, bridling. 'It's the ones on the outside with no one to look after them and nothin' to eat that're poor. I reckon this lot's the lucky ones.'

'And what are these people doing, master?' asked a clergyman, peering through the windows of the next shed, where old women and children were busily working on long, thick pieces of rope.

'They're pickin' oakum. Most of that rope comes from ships and they got to unravel it so's it can be made up again like new.'

'But that's an impossible task. That rope is full of knots and covered in tar.'

Blood shrugged. 'It's easy once you get the knack of it. Isn't it?' he shouted at a small girl sitting by the window, her fingers chaffed and bleeding.

'Yes, sir,' she whispered, not daring to look up. 'Easy.'

42

'Come in, Polly, come in,' Mrs Blood shouted at Clara. 'Don't stand in the doorway like a lump, girl.'

The shock of being forced to rise much earlier than usual had rattled the master's wife and she lumbered from one side of the bedroom to the other in her chemise and drawers, fretting and fuming.

'I don't know what to wear, I'm sure I don't,' she twittered, picking up a lace cap and throwing it down again. 'I can't seem to think straight. Shall I wear gloves or mittens?' She held a pair in each hand as if she were weighing them. 'So inconsiderate of the Guardians, so inconsiderate. They always give us at least a week's notice . . . I ought to have a fan. Where the devil is it?' she muttered, rummaging through a drawer. 'We're not their servants, indeed we're not. They can't expect us to jump whenever they snap their fingers. Or should I carry a parasol? Parasols are very fashionable, I hear. And

215

they'll want a big dinner. And who's got to arrange it? Who's got to send cook to market? Me!' She jabbed an angry finger at her substantial bosom. 'And they'll expect five or six courses. Oh yes, only the best for the Guardians. Shall I wear the green or the pink, I wonder?' She held up two dresses. The green was unusually restrained for her, with a high neckline, long sleeves and plain skirt. The pink was a jumble of frills, fringes, ribbons, bows and beads, with a dangerously low bodice and short puffed sleeves.

'The pink one, I think,' she said, admiring her reflection in the mirror. 'Mr Blood always compliments me when I wear pink and it does set off my complexion nice,' she simpered, holding the fabric up to her florid cheeks. 'Help me on with my corset, Polly. It's over there by the bed.'

This close-fitting undergarment was reinforced with strips of whalebone and metal designed to make the wearer's waist appear much smaller. As Mrs Blood was a large, formidable woman, her corset was equally large and formidable and Clara approached it with some trepidation.

'Well, pick it up, girl. Lor's sake, it won't bite you. Thread the laces through the eyelets,' said the master's wife, wrapping the corset around her ribs like a gigantic bandage, 'and get a move on. I never known nobody slow as you. I'm beginnin' to wish I'd still got Nell. She was a right chatterbasket but at least she was quick. She could lace up my corset like lightnin'. You done it yet?'

Clara fumbled with the laces while the master's wife kept up a steady barrage of instructions and abuse, but at last she had threaded them through the eyelets.

'Right. Now pull them tight. Tight as you can. Go on,' said Mrs Blood, holding on to the bedposts to give her better leverage.

Tentatively Clara took a lace in each hand and gave a tug.

'Tighter!' the woman urged her.

Clara gave another cautious tug.

'Blimey, you toerag, I'll never get that damned dress on if you don't get my corset tight enough,' exclaimed Mrs Blood, quite forgetting she was supposed to be a lady. 'Now pull. Hard as you can, girl. PULL!'

Lifting her hobnailed boot Clara put it firmly in the middle of Mrs Blood's broad back, grasped the laces and heaved on them with all her might, bending back and stretching out her leg as if she were reining in a team of cart horses. The eyelets almost met in the middle and Clara quickly tied the laces in a double knot.

The effect on Mrs Blood was dramatic. Her face turned scarlet and her eyes nearly popped out of her head.

'Aargh,' she gasped, jabbing a finger at the corset. 'Aargh.'

Until that moment Clara's movements had been slow and listless, her face devoid of expression, but the sight of Mrs Blood flailing her arms like a windmill and mouthing wordless threats at her galvanized the girl into action. She untied the knot, put her foot in the woman's back again and tugged even harder. This time the eyelets snapped together in a straight line. Clara retied the knot and stood back, arms folded, watching the master's wife with a wicked gleam in her eye as the woman struggled to breathe.

There was a discreet knock on the door and someone called out, 'Madam, Mr Blood says to tell you the Guardians've arrived and he's takin' them round the house.'

Mrs Blood stood quite still, her eyes glazed over, her mouth open, her tongue hanging out.

'Madam?' Another knock. 'Are you there?'

Mrs Blood let out a stifled squeak like a thin stream of air escaping from a balloon.

The orderly poked her head round the door, saw the stricken woman and shrieked, 'Lawks a mercy! You stupid girl –' she rounded on Clara – 'you tied her corset much too tight. Get her smellin' salts plaguy quick, they're in her reticule,' she said, releasing the master's wife from her whalebone prison. 'It's over there, child. Use your eyes!' She gave Clara a push. 'And you'd best make yourself scarce,' she added, as Mrs Blood sank to the floor. 'You'll be in for it when she comes round.'

43

Rats and mice scampered over Billy's scrawny body, darting up one trouser leg and down the other, searching his pockets for scraps of food and sniffing his fingers and toes. But apart from dislodging one that seemed intent on setting up home in his armpit and another that persisted in perching on his head, the little boy paid them scant attention.

The state of his stomach — the fact that it had received no sustenance for more than twenty-four hours — bothered him far more than any rodent. Even the memory of Mother Bailey's vile supper — the eclectic mix of dry crusts, apple cores, bones, the blackened remains of a cold baked potato, a half-chewed toffee, fish skins, a large lump of pastry that had obviously stuck to the sole of someone's boot and other delicacies — made Billy's mouth water.

44

'You ever been in the sewers, Captain?' Lanky asked as the two boys strode along.

'Yeh, dozens of times.'

'When?'

'When I was a nipper.'

'Why?'

'Cos I was a tosher.'

'What's that?'

'Someone that looks for tosh in the sewers.'

'What's tosh?'

'Things you can sell.'

'What kind of things?'

'Bits of metal, rope, bones, nails, knives, forks, spoons, cups, mugs, bits of jewellery – anythin' that'll bring in some of the ready. Sometimes, if I had a regular crow, I'd find coins. I found a sovereign once, only One-eyed Eric took it off me.'

'Who's One-eyed Eric?'

'The cove I used to work for before I took up crossin' sweepin'.'

'Why's he called One-eyed Eric?'

'Cos he's only got one eye.'

'Why's he only got one eye?'

'Cos he lost the other one.'

'What, you mean it fell out?'

'I don't know.'

'Where's he live?'

'Bermondsey?'

'*Bermondsey?* Crikey, that's the other side of the river.'

'I know.'

'So why we goin' to see him?'

'Lor', you do ask a lot of questions, Lanky,' Captain complained. 'If I'd known you were such a windbag I'd never have brought you along.'

'And I wish you hadn't neither,' muttered Lanky, but so low that Captain didn't hear him.

45

'Where we goin' now, Doug?' whispered Ned as the orderlies lined up the boys and marched them down the corridor.

'School.'

'School?' echoed Ned in horror. 'I never been to school. I don't know how to read nor write.'

'You won't have to. All we do is—'

'You talkin', Jones?' shouted one of the orderlies, bearing down on Doug.

'Nah, sir. I wasn't, sir. I was just clearin' my throat, sir. I got a frog in it, sir.'

'You'll have my fist in it if I hear another sound out of you.'

'Yeh, sir. Sorry, sir.'

The boys' schoolroom was as bleak and bare as every other room in the workhouse, with not a chair or table in sight. The only pieces of furniture were a large blackboard at one end, which looked so clean and shiny it was obvious it had never been used, the stocks, a painful device for punishing petty criminals, and a stool on which sat a loutish-looking young man with a birch cane under his arm.

'That's Zeke,' whispered Doug as the boys filed in and stood staring meekly at the floor. 'Blood's son. Even nastier than his old man, so watch out.'

'He our teacher?' asked Jem.

'Teacher?' Doug scoffed. 'He can't read nor write himself. Nah, we just stand here all mornin' doin' nothin' and if anyone—'

'You talkin' already, Jones?' shouted Zeke. 'Right, come out here. We might as well get the day off to a good start.' And with evident delight he clamped the boy's ankles and wrists in the stocks.

'Any other clack boxes want to join him?' he asked, looking round the room. 'You —' his eye fell on Jem — 'you new here?'

'Yeh.'

'What's your name?'

'Jem Perkinski.'

'Well, my name's sir, and you'd best remember it or . . .' Zeke swished the birch cane under Jem's nose. 'And what about the scarecrow next to you?'

'He's my brother Ned.'

The birch swished again, dangerously close to Jem's face.

'Sir,' said Jem without flinching.

'Well, Perkies, here's the rules. You stand there till the bell goes at midday and don't move and don't talk or I'll make you regret it. And straighten up, the lot of you!' he barked at the others. 'You look like sacks of coal.'

For the next two hours all the boys stood to attention, staring intently ahead, scarcely daring to blink for fear of being flogged or replacing Doug in the stocks.

The cuts on Jem's bottom were beginning to heal. And as they healed they tightened. And as they tightened they itched.

More than anything in the world Jem longed to ease his back, to stretch and bend it. And, above all, to scratch his bottom. So when he thought Zeke wasn't watching he began to slide his hand round inch by inch until he reached a particularly itchy bit.

It was the sigh of relief that gave him away.

'You moved, Perky,' said Zeke, striding down the room towards him.

'I couldn't help it. I—'

'Don't answer me back, you saucebox. I don't

like brats that answer me back. Go on, bend over,' snapped Zeke, raising the cane above his head. 'I'm goin' to learn you a lesson . . .'

But before he could do so, the door opened and an orderly came in carrying some books.

'What the . . . ?' Zeke spun round. 'What you doin' in here? Can't you see I'm busy, you stupe?'

'Master's orders, sir,' said the orderly. 'He says to tell you as how a load of nobs're comin' round and you got to learn the brats to read these.' And he put the books on the floor.

'Don't be soft,' sneered Zeke. 'The Guardians don't want us wastin' our time and their money learnin' this lot to—'

'It's not the guardians, sir,' the orderly interrupted him. 'Not the usual lot any road. These are swells, real rich people with titles – lawyers, politicians, clergymen. One's the Bishop of Bath and Wells.'

'Crimes!' exclaimed Zeke, turning white. 'What're they doin' here?'

'Makin' trouble for us, sir. Leastwise, that's what the master thinks.'

'These are my mum's books,' said Zeke, picking one up. 'She can read a bit. She'll help me. Where is she?' There was a note of panic in the young man's voice and his bullying attitude was rapidly disintegrating into that of an abject coward.

'Mrs Blood says to say she's in disposed, sir. Though I don't know where that is, I'm sure.' The orderly shrugged.

'All right, get out! I said, GET OUT!' Zeke shouted. Now —' he turned to the boys — 'can any of you read?'

The boys stood silently with heads bowed.

'Oh come on, there must be someone,' he whined.

Nobody moved.

'Oh please,' he pleaded. 'Just a few words. Surely one of you can.'

'I can,' piped up Jem, winking surreptitiously at Ned, who stared at him in amazement. 'I'm real sharp at readin'.'

Zeke snatched one of the books from the floor and opened it. 'Can you read what's on that page?' he said, thrusting the book at Jem.

'Course I can.'

'Well, go on then.'

'It says . . .' Jem frowned. 'Oh yeh, it says:

"Dirty days hath September
April, June and November.

From January up to May
The rain it raineth every day.
From May again until July
There's not a dry cloud in the sky.
All the rest have thirty-one
Without a blessed ray of sun.
And if any of them had two and thirty
They'd be just as wet – and quite as dirty."'

Ned had to dig his nails into his palms to stop himself laughing out loud, for their grandmother had taught them the verse, going over and over it until they knew it by heart, and at every family gathering either he or Jem was made to recite it. But Zeke was impressed.

'You take this book, Roberts, and you take this one, O'Reilly, and pretend to be readin' them when the toffs come in,' he instructed two of the boys. 'But if they ask anyone to read, you do it, Perky, all right?'

'Yeh, course I will.' Jem grinned. 'Sir.'

'And don't start whingin' to them neither,' said Zeke, releasing Doug from the stocks, 'or I'll thrash the livin' daylights out of the lot of you soon as they've gone.'

46

Kate at thirteen considered herself grown up, the eldest in the family, the apple of Pa's eye, a young woman with a respectable number of admirers and an important job serving gin and porter to the customers of the Dog and Bacon — and singing to them when they were too drunk to care. In short, a woman of the world, ambitious, industrious and confident — indeed some, including Gran, would have said she was downright cocky.

But when Ma took off after Goose on that sunny summer morning all Kate's bravado slipped away and she became a child again, half hoping Captain would come out and lead her to her brothers, half hoping he wouldn't. She wished Pa was there. She even wished Gran was there. But most of all she wished Jem, Ned and Billy were there, because then she wouldn't have had to go looking for the little pests.

'I'll wager this is all Jem's fault, as usual,' she

muttered to herself. 'The moment he was born I took one look at his ugly mug and knew he'd be an obstopolous little varmint – and he is. More trouble than he's worth – and he's not worth nothin'. And as for Ned . . . !'

And so she raged, using anger to mask the terrible unease she felt at being left alone in such a dangerous place.

As the day wore on, however, and hour after tedious hour trudged by with no sign of any activity in the lodging house, a weariness began to replace her initial anxiety. She whiled away the time humming snatches of songs, biting her fingernails, pulling lice out of her hair, scuffing her boots on the pavement and peering round the corner every now and then. But Captain did not appear, nor did anyone else, and at length, overcome by boredom and the stifling heat, Kate's eyes closed, her head sank on to her chest and sliding slowly down the wall she fell into a deep sleep.

47

'How much further is it?' said Lanky after he and Captain had walked along the streets parallel to the river for an hour or more.

'Far enough,' said Captain.

'I never been in this part of the world before,' said Lanky, looking around in wonderment as if he were in some foreign land. 'It's different, isn't it? It's—'

'Oy, there's someone I know,' Captain interrupted him, waving to a man at the end of the street. 'It's Short-armed Jake. He's a tosher too. Jake! Jake!'

The man stopped, saw Captain and waved back.

'What you doin' down here?' he called. 'I thought you were sweepin' dung in the Square?'

'I do,' said Captain, 'but I'm goin' to see One-eyed Eric.'

'Then you'd best turn round, son, cos he doesn't live in these parts no more, not since his accident.'

'What accident?' Captain frowned.

'Didn't you hear about it? He was workin' the sewers by himself – a soft thing to do, but you know what One-eyed Eric's like. Anyway, some rats flew at him unexpected and he lashed out at them and hit the wall by mistake and the whole thunderin' lot came down on him, broke him to pieces.'

Captain was shocked by the news. 'Poor bloke,' he said. 'So where's he livin' now?'

'A place off Water Street.'

'Where's that?'

'Between the Strand and the river.'

'Back there? Oh Lor'!' groaned Lanky. 'We've come all this way for nothin'.'

48

'And this,' said Blood, throwing open the door, 'is our schoolroom. Very proud of our little school we are. My son Zeke –' he put an arm round the young man's shoulders – 'teaches the boys to read and write and add up and take away and . . . and what else, Zeke?'

'A bit of history and jography and drawin', Dad,' said Zeke, with a modest smile. 'And we do a lot of singin' and dancin' too. They like that. Don't you?'

He narrowed his eyes at the boys and they nodded obediently.

'And what about the stocks?' enquired Miss Twine, pointing at them. 'Do the boys like them too?'

'They live a soft life here, so we keep the stocks to warn them what'll happen to them if they start misbehavin' when they leave. And what're you learnin' them today, Zeke?' asked Blood, eager to distract attention from the stocks.

'They're readin' poems, Dad.'

'Readin' poems, eh?' Blood repeated, just in case any of the visitors hadn't heard.

'Yeh, they're good at it, Dad. D'you want to hear one?'

'Well, I don't know if these ladies and gents have got the time, son,' said Blood, knowing full well what the answer would be.

'Of course we have,' said Sir Edmund. 'I'm sure we should be delighted to hear one of the boys reciting a poem.' And he turned to the members of the Visiting Society, who nodded their heads eagerly.

'All right,' said Zeke, relishing the chance to show off. 'You.' He handed Jem a book.

'What, me, sir?' said Jem, putting on a very bashful expression.

'Yeh.'

'But, sir—'

'Get on with it, will you?' snarled Zeke.

'Oh. Right, sir.' Jem opened the book, cleared his throat and began.

> "Dirty days hath September
> April, June and November.
> From January until May

234

The rain it falleth every day.
Then again until July
There's not a—"'

'Excuse me,' said Miss Twine, stepping forward. 'May I?' And she took the book out of Jem's hand. 'You were reading it upside down and . . . Oh!' She glanced at the cover. 'It's *Oliver Twist*. I don't recall Charles Dickens including that poem in his excellent book,' she said, trying desperately not to laugh.

'What is that disgusting smell, master?' enquired one of the ladies, covering her nose with a lace handkerchief as Blood hurried them out of the schoolroom, with a glance over his shoulder at Jem that should have felled the boy on the spot.

'Drains.' He pointed to the manhole cover in the courtyard. 'The sewage smells extra bad in hot weather like this, but you get used to it. Now, if you'd all be so good as to follow me up to the parlour, Mrs Blood just happens to have laid on a rattlin' spread – kidney puddin', pigeon pie, stewed rabbit, damson tart—'

'I thank you for your invitation, master, but we must be on our way. We are all busy people with

235

little time to spend eating lavish meals in the middle of the day,' said Sir Edmund icily. 'Why don't you give it to the inmates? Most of them look as if they haven't had decent food for years.'

'Oh, and Mr Blood,' said Miss Twine, 'what is the name of that boy who pretended he could read?'

'Jem P-Perkinski,' spluttered Blood, as if the name choked him.

'Jem Perkinski – I look forward to seeing him next time I'm here,' she said, giving Blood a meaningful look. He's such an amusing little fellow.

'Yeh,' growled Blood, 'he's very comical, he is.'

49

Ma was being led a merry dance around the streets of Holborn. Acting as suspiciously as any criminals, drawing close together and casting nervous glances over their shoulders, Goose and his little band of conspirators sped up one street and down the next, through alleyways and courtyards, under arches and over walls until the poor woman was panting.

'Slow down,' said Ruby. 'We'll lose her if we go on like this.'

'All right, everyone walk real slow for a bit so's she can catch us up,' instructed Goose. 'And then we'll—'

'Oy, watch where you're goin',' grumbled a man who was down on all fours drawing with coloured chalks on the flagstones. 'Now look what you've done, you clumsy varmint,' he complained as Goose stumbled over him. 'You've made me smudge his nose.'

'Sorry, guv. Who's it supposed to be?' said Goose,

bending down to take a closer look at the portrait the screever had drawn.

'It's Prince Albert. Anyone can see that,' said Ruby.

'That right, guv?' said Goose.

'Course not.' The screever laughed. 'It's the Iron Duke.'

The crossing sweepers looked at each other, perplexed.

'Don't tell me you've never heard of the Duke of Wellington?' said the screever, sitting back on his heels the better to admire his handiwork. 'He's famous, he is. He's the bloke that beat the Frenchies at the Battle of Waterloo.'

'Waterloo?' Goose shook his head in disbelief. 'There's never been no battle at Waterloo. I been over that bridge a hundred times and I never seen no froggies—'

'Not the bridge, you dunderhead,' laughed the screever. 'Waterloo's a place like London or . . . er . . . London. It's where they did all the fightin'.'

'So where is Waterloo, guv?' said Jack, summoning up the courage to ask a question.

'It's . . . er . . . somewhere in France.'

'And where's France?'

'Oh, a good few miles from here.' The screever waved his arm vaguely. 'Down by the sea.'

'What's the sea?'

'It's a lot of water.'

'Like a big puddle, you mean?'

'Bigger than that.'

'Like the Thames?'

'Nah, even bigger.'

'Paff!' Goose jeered. 'He's kiddin' you, Jack. There isn't no water bigger than the Thames.' And he walked away laughing.

A moment later Ma ran by, a worried expression on her face.

'Liza!' the screever called after her. 'Liza, what's wrong? Crushers after you, are they?'

'Oh, Joe —' Ma stopped — 'I didn't see you down there. I'm lookin' for some kids.'

'One of them got a kisser like this?' said the screever, running his finger from one ear to the other. 'And a girl with hair red as a radish?'

'Yeh.' Ma nodded eagerly. 'Which way'd they go?'

'Down Red Lion Street.'

50

Blood burst into the schoolroom just as Zeke was about to 'thrash Jem from here to Timbuktu for makin' me look a right stupe in front of all them toffs'.

'Leave off!' barked Blood. 'I got somethin' better in mind for that varmint.' He grabbed Jem by the ear and dragged him away. But Ned darted forward and hung on to Jem's arm.

'You're not takin' my brother nowhere,' he cried. 'You leave him alone.'

'Oh, so you want to come too, do you? Right!' said Blood, kicking Ned out the door. 'The more the merrier, my lad.'

51

'Where we goin' now, Goose?' said Ruby. 'I'm gettin' fed up with all this runnin' around.'

'And I'm hungry,' complained one of the other sweepers.

'Let's go home and get some grub.'

'Captain's sure to have got them kids out of the workhouse by now.'

'Yeh, Ruby's right. We're wastin' our time.'

'Let's go.'

'Come on—'

'Nah. Nah, wait a minute.' Goose held up his hands as the rebellious group made to run off. 'Let's have a bit of fun first.'

'Fun?' Ruby echoed in disgust. 'I don't want no fun. I want to go home.'

'We *are* goin' home,' insisted Goose, 'but we're goin' circumbendibus like.'

'Not me.' She pouted. 'I've had enough of goin' round in circles.'

'It's only a bit out of our way, just for a lark,' insisted Goose.

'Oh, I suppose so.' Ruby shrugged.

'Right, you cut along that way with Tilly.' He pointed to Hatton Garden. 'Spooney, you cut down Fetter Lane with Phil. Me and Danny'll go back along Holborn and—'

'Oh, I get it. That old haybag won't know which of us to follow,' giggled Ruby, taking a quick peek at Ma Perkinski, who was standing on the other side of the street pretending to listen to a man playing the hurdy-gurdy.

'But who'll I go with?' asked Jack in a plaintive voice.

Goose looked at the frail little boy doubtfully. 'You'll just have to keep up best you can,' he said.

'And don't let that woman catch you,' said Ruby.

'And if she does, don't tell her nothin',' said Spooney.

'Nothin', d'you hear?' said Danny.

Jack nodded meekly.

'Right, everybody.' Goose clapped his hands to get their attention. 'Ready? One, two, three . . . Go!'

In a flash the children split up and ran in all

directions. Ma spun round and her mouth fell open in dismay.

'Oy, missus,' the hurdy-gurdy man shouted after her as she sped away, 'you goin' to give me somethin'? I don't play for nothin', you know. I got to make a livin'. Women!' he muttered. 'Meanest creatures on earth.'

52

'There's a nice, quiet place for you,' cackled Blood, opening the door of the dead-house and pushing Jem and Ned ahead of him. 'Nobody'll bother you. And –' he pointed at the coffins – 'you certainly won't bother them.'

'You can't leave us in here with all them stiff'uns,' cried Jem, and wrenching himself free of Blood's grip he tried to make a bolt for it. But Blood caught him by the shoulder and sent him skittering across the floor.

'You'll stay there till you're a stiff'un yourself, my lad,' he snarled. 'And good riddance.' And muttering a string of oaths he locked and bolted the door and strode away.

'You all right, Jem?' whispered Ned.

'I skidded on my bum,' Jem said, rubbing it gingerly. 'I didn't have much skin on it anyway but it's all gone now. It must look like a nice bit of raw beef. Lucky Billy isn't here or he'd take a bite out of it,' he added with a grim attempt at humour.

'I am here, Jem,' came a small voice from the corner.

'Billy!' his brothers exclaimed as the little boy scrambled to his feet and ran towards them.

'I knew you'd come,' said Billy, jumping up and down excitedly. 'I knew you'd come and get me out.'

'We haven't,' said Ned.

'Course we have,' insisted Jem as Billy's face fell. 'We're goin' to get you out. We're all goin' to get out.'

'Oh yeh?' Ned muttered, casting a fearful glance at the coffins. 'How?'

'I'm workin' on it,' retorted Jem. 'Just give me a minute or two, will you?'

53

Kate woke with a start. Something had disturbed her, someone shouting.

She glanced at the thin ribbon of sky through the tops of the tenement houses. The sun had disappeared behind storm clouds. Her heart sank. She must have slept for hours; her mother would be furious if she knew. What if Captain had sneaked out while she was squatting against the wall, her eyes shut, dreaming? What if . . . ?

Again there was a shout.

Kate peeked round the corner. A newspaper boy was walking towards her waving copies of the *Standard*.

'Read all 'bout it!' he cried, although hardly anybody in Great White Lion Street could read, nor would they have wasted precious twopence on a newspaper. But the boy had had a poor day in the fashionable streets, for the intense heat had driven most people away, and so as he trudged home he hoped to entice someone with his lurid headlines.

'Read all 'bout it! Cholera kills two thousand! Ship goes down – all lives lost! Headless body found in well! Killer Kelly arrested! Runaway horse tramples woman and kids!'

Kate shot out of her hiding place and grabbed the boy's ragged sleeve. 'What did you say?'

'I said, runaway horse tramples—'

'Nah, before that. About Killer Kelly.'

'He's been arrested.'

'But why? Why?'

'He came out of the Coach and Horses on St Martin's Lane, lushy as usual, and gave a couple of crushers a right anointin', left them for dead. They reckon he'll get six months for it, maybe more, on account of one of the crushers was a sergeant – or it might have been an inspector. Here, why don't you read all about it?' said the boy, offering her a newspaper.

'Nah, why should I? You just told me all about it,' said Kate. And she skipped away, light of heart.

With Killer Kelly behind bars, Pa was out of danger, they could all go back to Devil's Acre, she could go back to work at the Dog and Bacon, Pa could go to the market again, Gran could tell fortunes and sell her magic potions again, Ma could . . .

Kate stopped skipping. Where was Ma? She'd been gone all day. Had she found Jem, Ned and Billy?

'Must tell Pa,' Kate said out loud. 'Must get Pa plaguy quick.'

And she set off at a run.

54

The workhouse was buzzing with the news of Mrs Blood's mishap.

'Polly Parrot,' the inmates whispered to each other, 'nearly finished off the old trout.'

'Nearly?'

'Yeh.'

'Pity.'

By the time she got back to her ward Clara was a heroine.

'Is it true?' The girls crowded round her. 'Did you hear her ribs crack?' said Hope. 'Did her eyes pop out?' said Faith. 'Did her tongue turn black?' said Charity.

Clara tried to walk away but they followed her, bombarding her with questions. 'Did she scream? . . . Did she send for a crusher . . . Oh, come on, Polly, tell us, say somethin'.'

'All right, that's enough shindig, you lot!' snapped an orderly, pushing them aside. 'Get in a

line and quick about it. And you, Polly. You can do a bit of oakum pickin' too – though from what I hear, if Mrs Blood has her way, it'll be the last thing you ever do on this earth.' She sniggered.

55

One-eyed Eric's new home was a garret overlooking a grimy courtyard. When Captain and Lanky arrived a vigorous fight was in progress between two women, and the boys had to barge through the hundreds of cheering onlookers, all of whom lived, at least ten or twelve to a room, in the ramshackle houses that surrounded the courtyard.

One-eyed Eric had been a strong man with a florid complexion, bright eyes and the kind of expression that made less robust mortals quake. But the accident in the sewers had left him crippled, his legs shattered, his mind embittered.

'You come to crow, have you?' he greeted Captain sourly as the boy entered the miserable room where the former tosher sat confined to a chair, gazing out of the window for hours on end.

'Nah, I need your help,' said Captain.

'Help?' The man grunted. 'I'm no help to nobody no more. No help to myself. No help to her.' He nodded at his wife, who was snoring in a corner, an empty gin bottle in her hand. 'And as for my boy, Joe – d'you know what he's doin'? D'you know what that half-baked, knocker-faced dolt's doin'?'

Captain shook his head. He didn't know and he didn't want to, but he had a feeling One-eyed Eric was going to tell him anyway.

'Works as a screever – that's a highfalutin name for a ninny that draws pictures on the pavement in chalk. Can you believe it? My son, my only child, scribbles on the pavement!'

'Eric, I—' Captain began.

'*I* was a tosher, my *dad* was a tosher, my *granddad* was a tosher. And we were proud of it.'

'Eric, I want—'

'It's a decent, honourable profession. You got to be up to snuff to be a tosher. You got to be plucky. You got to be sharp.'

'Eric, I want to—'

'You got to be a man, not a booby messin' about with chalks.'

'Eric, I want to get—'

'I said to his mum, you give Joe chalks, I said, you give Joe chalks to play with and you'll be sorry.'

'Eric, I want to get into—'

'But nah, she wouldn't listen to me. Encouraged

him, she did. Draw them pretty pictures, Joe, she said.'

'Eric, I want to get into the—'

'So now he draws pretty pictures on the pavement instead of doin' a proper job like me and his granddad and his great-granddad and his—'

'Eric, I want to get into the sewers.'

'What?' One-eyed Eric's one eye stared at Captain in amazement. 'What for? There's no money in it no more. There was a time I'd come home with a couple of sovereigns a day, but now I'd be lucky to get a few bob. Nah, you don't want to waste your time bein' a tosher, son.'

'I don't want to be a tosher,' Captain protested. 'I just want to get into the Strand Workhouse.'

'You could try the front door,' said One-eyed Eric drily. 'It'd be a lot easier.'

'I can't. I got to get some kids out.'

'Small kids, are they?'

'One of them's . . .' Captain held out his hand to show how small Billy was.

One-eyed Eric shook his head. 'He'd never make it.'

'I was no bigger than him when I worked the sewers.'

'Yeh, but you were with me.'

'Eric, we got to do it. We got to get them boys out before a couple of women get there and nab them.'

'What about him?' The man pointed at Lanky. 'He been down the sewers before?'

'Nah, never.'

'Does he know what it's like?'

'Nah, and he doesn't want to neither.'

But before Captain could stop him, One-eyed Eric had launched into a vivid description of the filthy, stinking pipes and passages, tubes and tunnels, crypts and cellars hidden beneath the streets of London.

'It's not so much the smell, though that can make you cough and choke a bit, and sometimes the air's so bad it explodes . . . nah, it's the wadin' through all that muck and not knowin' what's goin' to happen. One minute your feet's on solid ground and the next – if you don't know your way around like me and the other toshers do – you step in a hole and before you can say Hell'n Tommy you're up to your eyeballs and drownin' fast.

'Then there are the rats, millions of them. Your sewer rat is brown, on account of it comes from Germany, and devilish fierce. It'll jump at your throat soon as look at you. That's what happened to

me,' he said ruefully. 'And it pees in the water –
which is fair enough, we all do – only when rat's pee
gets into your cuts and scratches it gives you West's
disease, which ends up in your brain and sends you
stark ravin' looney.

'And talkin' of looneys –' One-eyed Eric was
warming to his subject – 'you'll see a lot of them
down there. Escaped from Bedlam, they have,
along with thieves and murderers hidin' from the
law. And talkin' of escapin' – ' one subject seemed
to flow smoothly into the next in One-eyed Eric's
mind – 'there's a herd of boars roamin' around.
They're huge, fierce pigs that ran away from the
slaughterhouse and got into the sewers and went
wild. I've never seen them myself,' he added regretfully, 'cos they're up Hampstead way. I never seen
the crocodiles neither, though I've looked, cos they
say they're guardin' a treasure, a ton of gold or silver and I'd've liked to get my hands on that.

'Then there are the dragons. You don't want to
meet up with them. Horrible they are, with horns
and teeth sharp as daggers. What's up with him?' He
frowned as Lanky slumped to the floor, his face
ashen, his eyes swivelling wildly in his head.

'I think he's feelin' a bit all-overish on account of

the heat,' said Captain, propping Lanky against the wall.

'Throw a bucket of water over him,' suggested One-eyed Eric helpfully.

'You got one?' said Captain, looking round the room.

'Nah, you'll have to go down to the tap. There's one on the corner, only it hasn't been workin' for a couple of days. Here, give him some of this,' he said, pulling a bottle of gin from his pocket. 'Just a sip.'

Captain tipped the bottle and poured gin into Lanky's slack mouth. The boy coughed and spluttered back to life and looked round the room vacantly. But on catching sight of One-eyed Eric he suddenly recalled where he was and scrambling to his feet he made for the door.

'You goin' somewhere?' demanded Captain.

'Yeh, home,' shouted Lanky, who was halfway down the stairs.

'Oh? You got a home, have you?'

Lanky hesitated.

Captain gave a sardonic chuckle.

With a deep, gut-wrenching sigh, Lanky dragged himself back into the room.

'I don't reckon he's up to it,' said One-eyed Eric.

'Course he is. We won't have no problems,' said Captain confidently.

'If you say so.' The man shrugged. 'You'll be all right long as you remember to keep together all the time. If one of you gets lost he's done for. A lot of people've died wanderin' round and round them sewers. And don't touch the walls or ceilin's, cos they're so worn the lot'll fall on you – like they did me,' he said in a bitter voice, glancing at his crippled legs. 'And watch the water. Now they've put them gates over the openings to the river the tide can't rush up like it used to, but a rainstorm can come on awful quick. The water flows down the gutters and fills the sewers and before you know it it's on you like a ton of bricks. I've seen it knock grown men over and—'

'Rain?' Captain snorted. 'We haven't had no rain for months.'

One-eyed Eric beckoned him to the window. 'See them,' he said, pointing to black clouds above the rooftops. 'Full of water, they are. It's a dangerous time to go down the sewers, lad.'

'But we got to go now, Eric. We got to.'

'All right, it's your funeral. Here, take my pole and that.' He indicated a large bag on the floor.

'What do I want that for?'

257

'Case you find anythin', of course. And put that belt on. Right, now stick the light in it,' he said, pointing to a bullseye lantern. 'And remember to turn it off when you pass under a gratin' in the street or people'll see you and tell a crusher. They get five bob for snitchin' on us since they made it against the law to go down the sewers. They say it's cos they're worried about our health,' he said, flushing with anger. 'Course, they're not worried about us not bein' able to earn money and starvin' to death. That don't matter. Oh no, as long as we're—'

'Where's the best place to get in, Eric?' said Captain, stopping him before he could get going on what was obviously one of his favourite gripes. 'I never been in any of the sewers up this end of the river. You and me used to work that one in Bermondsey when you lived on Pickle Herring Street.'

'Yeh, I miss it. We had some happy times down there, didn't we?' he said, looking at Captain fondly, for he had always had a soft spot for the boy and wished his own son could have been more like him. 'But when I did this –' he tapped his legs – 'I had to move up here with Joe. I can get Long Tom to help you, though. He lives over there.' He nodded towards a window on the other side of the court-yard. 'Been a tosher as long as me — knows the sewers like the back of his hand. Tom!' he hollered, cupping his hands around his mouth. 'Tom! You there, you lushy old varmint?'

Moments later a face appeared at the window.

'What d'you want?'

'You got to help a young mate of mine.'

'And what'll I get for it?'

One-eyed Eric held up the gin bottle.

'I'll be right there.' Long Tom grinned.

56

Ma had no hope of following the older children. By the time she got to Gray's Inn Lane they were long gone, but she could see Jack scurrying down Holborn and she set off in hot pursuit.

'Just wait till I get my hands on you, you toerag. Just wait!' she muttered as she panted along, for she had realized too late that the crossing sweepers had led her on a wild goose chase.

Jack ran as quickly as he could, his bare feet pounding the pavement, but he was tired after the day's exertions. Slower and slower he went, barging into people, tripping over crates and boxes outside shops, as Ma gained on him.

At the crossroads of King Street and Queen Street the traffic was dense. Hansom cabs vied for space with carriages and carts, the drivers swearing and cracking their whips at each other.

Jack hesitated, but only for a moment, and then blindly, foolishly, he rushed into the road.

'Look out there!' yelled the driver of a hansom, swerving to avoid him, but as the back wheel swung round it caught the boy and sent him sprawling into the gutter, where he lay dazed and breathless.

Ma leaped on him before he could stagger to his feet and cried, 'Where are my boys?'

Jack stared up at her, ashen-faced.

'I said, where are my boys? Where're Jem, Ned and Billy?' She took him by the shoulders and shook him. 'Tell me! Tell me!'

'I-I don't know, m-missus.'

'Don't lie to me. Don't lie or I'll—'

'I c-can't tell you,' stammered Jack, trying to wriggle out of her grasp.

'Why not? I'm their mother.'

'Nah.' Jack shook his head. 'Nah, you're not. We know you're not.'

'Don't be a ninny. Course I am.'

Again Jack shook his head.

Ma was so frustrated she raised her hand to hit him. But then she had a better idea and grabbing the little boy by the collar she ran back along Holborn dragging him with her.

'Where we goin'?' Jack cried in terror, for he now thought he himself was being kidnapped. 'Where you takin' me?'

The screever was just starting on a portrait of Napoleon when Ma arrived with Jack struggling and screaming.

'So you found one of them, my china?' He laughed.

'Yeh, I did,' said Ma, grim-faced. 'Tell this little varmint who I am, Joe. Tell him who my old man is and my boys.'

'Your old man's Bert the Beast, Liza. Everyone knows that. And your boys are Jem, Ned and Billy.'

Jack stopped screaming and looked at Ma in amazement.

'But . . . but we thought you were snatchers, missus. We thought you were goin' to nab them boys.'

Ma sat back on her heels, stunned. 'But *I* thought *you'd* nabbed them.'

'Nah, we haven't got them.'

'So . . . so where are they?'

'They're in the Strand Workhouse. That's where they are.'

'*The Strand?*' All the blood drained from Ma's face. 'Oh, Lor', not with Blood, not that monster.'

'It's all right, missus,' said Jack, as she got to her feet. 'Captain's gone to get them. He and Lanky are . . .'

But Ma had gone, running like the wind.

57

Kate ran all the way back to the yard near Hungerford Market and when she got there she had the stitch so badly she could barely speak.

'What's up, my tulip?' cried Pa, almost falling down the steps of the caravan in his haste. 'Somethin' happened to Ma? Is it the boys? Is it . . . ?'

'K-Killer Kelly,' gasped Kate, bending double.

Thinking that Kate meant Killer Kelly was in hot pursuit, Pa rushed into the caravan, nearly knocking Gran off the step, and came out wielding a cosh.

'Nah . . . nah, Pa,' said Kate. 'He's not here. He's in prison . . . or soon will be.' And, pausing every now and then to get her breath, she told him what the newspaper seller had said.

'Lor', that's a jammy bit of news, my lovely, and no flies,' chortled Pa, hugging her. 'But —' his face fell — 'what about Ma and Jem and Ned and Billy?'

'Some varminty crossin' sweepers've nabbed the boys, Pa. Ma went after them this mornin' and left me to keep watch but –' Kate hung her head – 'I fell asleep.'

Pa frowned. 'So you don't know where your ma is?'

'Nah.'

'And where do these crossin' sweepers hang out?'

'Seven Dials. A crummy paddin' ken in Great White Lion Street.'

'Right,' said Pa, pulling on his cap. 'I think I'll go and have a word with them.

58

'That wretched Polly near finished me off, Mr Blood. Strangulated me, she did,' fumed his wife. 'I want her punished, d'you hear? I want you to bring her here right now and—'

'I will, dearest, course I will. But I think we should have dinner first,' said Blood, who was greedy as well as cruel.

'Dinner? How can you think about eatin' when I'm sufferin'?'

'You got to keep body and soul together, dearest. You got to build up your strength. And it'd be a shame to let all this grub get cold. Them toffs don't know what they're missin'. Workhouse Visitin' Society be damned! They'd best not stick their noses in here again or they'll regret it.'

'But Polly—'

'Will be dealt with directly we've finished, dearest. She can't run away. Where would she run to?' He laughed. 'Now, let's sit down and enjoy our dinner, shall we?'

But Mrs Blood was in such an agitated state after her misadventure with the corset that her devoted husband had to persuade her to eat.

'Do try, dearest. Just a morsel,' he coaxed her, ripping the leg from a rabbit and putting it on her plate. 'You must keep your strength up.'

'I'm that vexed I can't hardly swallow,' she complained, tearing at the meat with strong, sharp teeth. 'She knew what she was doin', that little minx. Looked right at me, she did, and smirked. And me near swoonin', Mr Blood.'

'Don't, dearest,' he beseeched her. 'It hurts me just thinkin' about it. Have some of this kidney puddin'.'

'I couldn't, Mr Blood, I really couldn't. Well, maybe a spoonful or two and some potatoes and hot peas. Oh, when I think of that wretched girl!'

'Don't distress yourself, dearest. I'll deal with her. More wine?' he said, refilling her glass for the third time.

'You'll flog her, Mr Blood?'

'She won't have a shred of skin left on her body by the time I'm finished with her, dearest.'

'You'll give her a black eye?'

'Two, dearest. And a bloody nose, if you'll forgive the expression.'

'You'll tear out her fingernails?'

'And her toenails. Do try a little of the pigeon pie, dearest. More wine?'

59

To prevent the high tide from filling the sewers and rising through the gratings to swamp the streets of London with foul-smelling ordure, the Sanitary Commissioners had built a strong brick wall within the entrance to all the sewers along the Thames. In each of these walls there was an opening covered by an iron door suspended from the top, which swung open to allow water and sewage out but was forced shut to prevent the rising tide from getting in. As a by-product of this ingenious device the Commissioners also intended to stop toshers from getting into the sewers, but they had reckoned without the resourcefulness and determination of these hardy men who, despite the hazards and the prospect of being arrested and imprisoned, still waded through the filthy tunnels searching for anything of value.

Long Tom was just such a man, tough and taciturn. Dressed in the uniform of a tosher, a canvas apron, canvas trousers and long, greasy velveteen coat with huge pockets, he led Captain and Lanky down to the river.

'Tide's low. Good,' he said when they got to the sewer entrance. 'Come on. And don't lift your feet up, just slide them along the bottom so's you can feel your way.'

Wordlessly the two boys followed him into the dark tunnel. Cold, grey slurry swirled around their knees, forcing them back, and although they were used to foul smells the reek from the outpourings of London's 200,000 cesspits made them gasp.

'Keep close,' whispered Captain.

'I am,' said Lanky through clenched teeth.

Their voices echoed eerily through the tunnel and giant shadows on the walls stalked them like phantoms.

'Blimey!' shrieked Lanky as something bumped against his legs. 'What's that?'

Long Tom and Captain turned and in the dull glow of their candle lanterns the boy saw the bloated body of a dead dog.

'Plenty of them,' said the tosher. 'Men and women too. Murdered. Chucked down here.'

Eels, bigger than any the boys had ever seen in the fish markets, slithered through the murky

269

depths and toads and frogs watched them pass with bulging eyes and gulping throats.

'They won't last long,' said Long Tom, 'not when the rats get them.'

Rats. They were everywhere. Running along the ledges, scampering in and out of the holes in the brickwork, pausing now and then to watch the three intruders with sharp, inquisitive eyes.

'Don't like gettin' their feet wet,' Long Tom chuckled. 'Not if they can help it.'

'There aren't arf a lot of them,' muttered Lanky.

'They got to live best way they can, just like the rest of us.'

After a while Lanky lost all sense of reality. The breath-stopping smells, the unearthly blackness, the startling splash whenever something plopped into the water, the unending procession of decaying objects that bobbed past unhinged his mind and he began to feel he was wading through a hideous nightmare that would never end.

'Big hole here,' Long Tom warned them. 'Keep to this side.' But Lanky, as if in a trance, staggered straight on and was suddenly up to his waist and sinking fast.

'Guv!' shouted Captain.

'Stay back!' Long Tom ordered him. And holding out his pole he said, 'Grab it!' to Lanky and began to pull him out of the quagmire.

'He's no use, Captain,' he said bluntly when Lanky was on safer ground again. 'He'd best go back.'

'Nah, I can't go b-back,' stammered Lanky, petrified at the thought of finding his way through the gruesome tunnel on his own. 'I haven't got no light. I haven't got no—'

'I'll go with you. Wait here. Come on, Captain, I'll show you where you got to turn off for the workhouse.'

Leaving a shivering Lanky, Captain and Long Tom set off and after a short time the tunnel opened out and they were at a junction with many tunnels branching off in all directions.

'That one.' Long Tom pointed with his pole at a dark, forbidding hole to their left. 'Go down it about a quarter-mile, you'll see a ladder. That goes up into the workhouse yard.'

'Thanks, guv,' said Captain as cheerfully as he could, although his heart failed him at the thought of going on alone.

'Take care, lad,' said the man, his expression grim. 'If you fall down, use the pole to pull you up again. And if your lantern goes out, run the other way plaguy quick cos it means the air's so bad it'll kill you.'

And with that dire warning he was gone.

60

The master and his wife had demolished the best part of a rabbit, kidney pudding, pigeon pie, damson tart and raspberry biscuits liberally washed down with wine. And more wine. And more wine.

Bloated and belching they finally lay down their knives and forks and fell into a drunken stupor, Blood's head resting on the table, his arms hanging limply by his sides, his wife sprawling in her chair, her mouth wide open, a dribble of saliva trickling down her chins.

An orderly knocked on the door and called out, 'Can I clear away now, madam?'

On receiving no reply but a barrage of tonsil-wrecking, nostril-ripping snores, she opened the door and peered round it.

'Blimey,' she muttered when she saw the drunken pair, 'they'll have sore heads when they come round.'

And she closed the door softly behind her and tiptoed away.

61

'I'm so hungry, Jem,' whined Billy. 'My belly's killin' me.'

'So's mine.'

'And I'm thirsty.'

'Me too.'

'D'you reckon they'll give us any grub?'

'Course they will. I'll wager Blood's missus is cookin' it for us herself – a nice dish of pigs' trotters, some mutton pies, a big baked potato, rhubarb tart and . . .'

'Stow it, Jem!' growled Ned.

'And some Chelsea buns and brandy balls and—'

'I said, stow it!'

'And a nice sprinklin' of rat and mouse droppin's over the lot. There's nothin' like rat and mouse droppin's for flavour.'

62

Blood woke from his drunken sleep some hours later with bloodshot eyes, trembling hands and a head full of stampeding buffalo.

'Orderlies!' he bellowed. 'Orderlies!'

'Mr Blood, please!' His wife came to with a grunt and a snort. 'I'd be exceedin' obliged if you would keep your voice down. I'm in a delicate state, what with bein' brutally crushed and bruised,' she grumbled, although it was the mounds of food and gallons of alcohol that had made her unwell, and not a too tight corset. 'I think I'll take to my bed,' she said and made to get up. But the effort was too much and she fell back in her chair with a groan.

'Well, help the mistress, you fools!' Blood snapped at the orderlies.

'Gently, gently,' she admonished them as they heaved her out of her chair. 'Remember my poor ribs. And, Mr Blood?'

'Yes, dearest?'

'I don't never want to see that wicked Polly ever again. Do I make myself clear?'

'Perfectly clear, dearest.' Blood nodded. 'There's no place in this world for vicious creatures the likes of her. You,' he grunted at two more orderlies hovering in the doorway, 'go and find Polly Parrot . . . Well, don't just stand there,' he shouted as the men shifted from one foot to the other, exchanging nervous glances. 'Go and find her. NOW!'

'Er . . . Yeh, guv . . . but, er . . . but what'll we do with her when we find her?'

'Put her in the dead-house with the other pesky brats. They can all rot together.'

63

Goose and the crossing sweepers were tucking into their usual meal of street droppings, which Mother Bailey had left for them, she having gone to visit her daughter who had just given birth to her twelfth baby.

'Jack's not back yet,' said Ethel.

'Wonder if that woman got him?'

'I'll wager she did.'

'Yeh, and he'll have told her everythin',' Ruby said in disgust.

'Nah, Jack wouldn't do that.' Ethel shook her head.

'He would!' said Ruby, her auburn ringlets jiggling crossly.

'Yeh, Ruby's right, we shouldn't've left him.' Phil nodded agreement.

'I kept sayin' that,' said Ruby, getting angrier by the minute. 'I kept sayin' it, but nobody never lis—'

Goose, who was busily licking the last of the revolting gruel from his bowl, was taken aback when Ruby stopped in mid-sentence, since her tirades usually went on for some time. He glanced up, saw the expression on her face and turned his head to see what had unnerved her.

A giant of a man stood in the doorway, a fierce expression on his face and an evil-looking cosh in his hand.

'I got a crow to pick with you,' he growled.

Goose swallowed hard. In Captain's absence he was in charge, but he wished at that moment that he wasn't. 'Who are you?' he asked.

He knew the answer even before the man ducked his head under the lintel, stepped into the kitchen and said, 'I'm Albert Perkinski, known to one and all as Bert the Beast. You've probably heard of me.'

The children nodded mutely, keeping a close eye on the cosh.

'I hear you've got my boys – Jem, Ned and Billy,' said Pa.

'I told you they were his kids,' Ruby hissed in Goose's ear. 'I kept sayin'—'

Goose was outraged. 'You did not!' he exclaimed. 'You said—'

'I didn't! I said—'

'Enough of that!' snapped Pa. 'Where are they?'

'They're in the Strand Workhouse, mister.'

Pa let out a gasp, as if he'd been punched in the stomach. 'Lawks a mercy!' he exclaimed.

'Nah, it's all right, mister. Captain and Lanky've gone to get them out.'

'And who're they?'

'Captain's leader of the TSCS . . . the TCDS . . . us crossin' sweepers,' explained Goose. 'And Lanky's . . . well, he's Lanky.'

'You mean they're just kids?'

'Nah,' protested Goose, offended. 'Captain's fourteen.'

'But they can't get my boys out of no workhouse. Only their ma or me can do that.'

'Yeh, well, we didn't think they had no ma nor pa, so Captain's gettin' them out another way.'

'What other way?'

'Through the sewers.'

For the second time Pa looked as if he'd received a vicious blow in a painful place.

'Captain knows his way round them,' Goose reassured the distraught man. 'He used to work for One-eyed Eric when he was a nipper. We didn't mean your kids no harm, mister,' Goose called after

Pa as he hurried away. 'We were just tryin' to help them. We thought some women were after them.'

Pa hesitated. 'Was one of them about this high,' he held his hand halfway up his vast ribcage, 'with grey hair and a boater with no brim and the other one a girl with ginger hair and freckles?'

'Yeh.' Ruby pushed Goose aside in her eagerness to tell Pa. 'A couple of ugly customers, mister. I could see they were up to no good the minute I clapped eyes on them.'

'You never saw them,' said Goose.

'I did,' protested Ruby. 'I saw them clear as day.'

'Ugly customers, were they?' said Pa.

'Ugliest I ever seen.' Ruby nodded.

'They're my missus and my girl,' said Pa.

Ruby's face turned as red as her hair. 'Oh,' she muttered as the other sweepers jabbed each other in the ribs and sniggered.

But Pa said, 'Well, I got to thank you all for tryin' to help my boys. Your hearts are in the right place even if your brains are a bit askew.' And reaching into his pocket he put twopence on the table, turned on his heel and was gone.

64

Captain was not a coward. Many times he had stood up to people stronger than him, especially when he thought he or one of the other crossing sweepers was being treated unfairly, and he had once thrashed a man for ill-treating a horse. But as he stood knee deep in the stinking water listening to the 'swish, swish' of Long Tom's canvas trousers as he waded away, his courage began to fail him and he longed to run after the tosher, to get out into the sunlight, to breathe freely again.

'*What're you doin' down here, you blockhead?*' demanded a small, insistent voice in his head.

'I got to find Jem, Ned and Billy. I got to help them.'

'*Why? They're nothin' to you. You've only known them a few hours.*'

'But I promised to—'

'*Promised? Paff! That doesn't mean nothin'. People break promises all the time.*'

'But me and Jem swore an oath. That means we're brothers.'

'Don't talk bosh! Go on, get out of here while you can. If you move fast you'll catch Long Tom.'

'Oh, drat!' Captain cried out in anguish as the battle between loyalty and cowardice waged back and forth in his head.

'Oh, drat, drat, drat!' The word reverberated eerily around the tunnels. *'Oh, drat, drat, brat!'*

'Oy!' Captain exclaimed. 'None of that!'

'That, that, that!' mocked the echo. *'That, that, brat!'*

Captain was incensed. Even though common sense told him the mocking voice was his own and the apparent insult was simply a distortion of the sound as it grew fainter, he clenched his fists, finding some relief from his fear in anger, and yelled, 'I am not a brat! I'm captain of the crossin' sweepers and proud of it. So shut your trap!'

'Trap, trap, trap!' The voice echoed its ominous warning as Captain turned into the black tunnel that led to the workhouse, moving very slowly, prodding the ground ahead of him and not taking a step until he was absolutely sure it was safe.

This side tunnel was narrower than the main one and after a while Captain began to feel the sweaty walls were closing in on him. The rats were more numerous here too and, now that he was on his own, more daring. One nipped at his elbow and he lashed at it with his pole, swearing. The end of the pole caught the side of the lantern attached to his belt and nearly dislodged it. Captain froze, cursing himself for a fool. Without a light he'd be done for. He would stumble through the blackness until he died of starvation or choked on noxious gases or was attacked and devoured by wild boars or crocodiles or dragons or . . .

'Nah, it isn't true,' he said out loud to comfort himself. 'There isn't nothin' like that down here. One-eyed Eric was just makin' it up.'

There was a loud splash close behind him.

'Oh, Lor'!' he whispered. 'It's a crocodile! It's a dragon! It must've heard me. It's comin' after me.'

Every muscle in his body screamed at him, 'Run! Run!' But he knew that would be foolish. If he moved too quickly he would fall into a hole and disappear in a moment. No, he had to stand and face the creature, whatever it was.

Grasping the pole firmly with both hands, he turned and peered down the tunnel. Something was swimming towards him. He could see its head, a small, grey head making waves as it cut through the water. Not a crocodile then. Not a wild boar or

a dragon. Something smaller. A lizard? Could lizards swim? A snake? Oh no – he shrank back in horror – not a poisonous snake.

It was moving fast, coming straight at him. He could see its beady eyes glittering in the lamplight.

He raised his pole high above his head, his hands sweating so much it nearly slipped out of his grasp.

It was nearly on him now, just a few yards more.

He brought the pole down, slamming it on the water again and again in a frenzy.

The creature veered away and climbing on to the ledge shook itself vigorously. Then it crouched down, blinking water out of its eyes and let out a piteous, 'Miaow'.

65

'Crikey, at this rate we'll have the whole of London here in a minute,' said Jem as the door of the dead-house opened and a small girl was thrown in.

'Who is it?' said Ned.

'How the devil do I know?'

Clara had been on the point of bursting into tears, for the orderlies had thrown her so violently she had banged her head against one of the coffins. But she sat up, peering into the gloom.

'Who're you?' demanded Jem.

'Jem, is that you?' said Clara. Elated at hearing a familiar voice she had suddenly found her own again. 'Oh! Oh, I can talk!' she cried in delight. 'I can talk!'

'Yeh, sounds like it,' said Jem drily. 'But who *are* you?'

'I'm Clara.'

'Clara? What, the crossin' sweeper? What you doin' in here?'

Quickly the girl told them how she had been arrested and condemned to the workhouse and the boys listened and nodded sympathetically. But when she got to the part where she had nearly asphyxiated the master's wife with her own corset they were doubled up with laughter.

'You're a sharp one,' said Jem admiringly.

'Yeh, and now I'm bein' punished for it,' said Clara. 'Them pesky orderlies said I'd stay in here till I was nothin' but a pile of bones. What is this place, anyway?'

'It's the . . .' began Jem, but at that moment the moon slid out from behind the clouds and a shaft of light illuminated the dead-house, shining eerily on the coffins stretched in a neat row against the wall.

Clara, who had been resting her back against one, gave a scream and scrambled away.

'They're only stiff'uns,' said Jem. 'They can't hurt you.'

'They can!' protested Billy. 'When it gets dark, real dark, they come back to life and go lookin' for kids so's they can grab our bodies. Then they jump in and shove us out so then we're dead and go to hell instead of them.'

'Who told you that load of hornswoggle?' sneered Jem.

'You did.'

Jem was glad no one could see his face clearly for it had turned an embarrassing shade of scarlet. 'Yeh . . . well, we're just wastin' time chatterin' about nothin' when we should be thinkin' about how we're goin' to get out of here,' he said.

'What d'you mean *we*?' said Ned. 'You said *you* were thinkin' about it. You said, "Give me a minute or two," and that was hours and hours ago.'

'All right, all right, I have thought.'

'Well?'

'Well . . . we . . . uhm . . . We . . .' Jem glanced up at the roof, hoping for inspiration. 'We get out there,' he said, pointing at the hole in the tiles.

Ned followed his gaze.

'We'll never get out through a hole that small. Anyway, how'd we get up there? Fly?'

'We'll use them coffins.'

'How?'

'Put one on top of the other and climb up.'

'But they're too heavy to move. They've got stiff'uns in them.'

'Not them ones, you fathead. The empty ones. Come on, let's get started.'

Turning the first coffin over, they lifted the second on top of it, leaving just enough room for

288

their feet, and so on until all the coffins made a very steep staircase. Fortunately the roof of the dead-house was so low that only six coffins were needed to reach it, and Blood's stinginess worked in the boys' favour for once, because the coffins were made of such thin wood they were quite light.

'That's jammy!' said Jem, well content with his handiwork. 'We'll be out on the roof as fast as ninepence. Go on up, Ned, and when you get to the top—'

'Oh,' said Ned, bristling, 'why've I got to go first?'

'Well, somebody's got to.'

'I reckon we should draw for it.'

'Crimes!' Jem exclaimed in exasperation. 'Oh, all right. Clara, take this,' he said, pulling a splinter off one of the coffins, 'and put both hands behind your back. Ned, you got to guess which hand she's got it in.'

Ned frowned and said, 'Left . . . Nah, right . . . Nah, le . . . Nah, ri . . .'

'Get on with it, Lor's sake!' grumbled Jem. 'I'm not standin' here all night listenin' to you sayin' "Le . . . Nah, ri . . . Nah, le . . . Nah, ri . . ."'

'Right . . . Nah, left, left,' said Ned, his mind finally made up.

'Left it is,' said Clara, holding out her hand.

'Up you go then, Ned,' said Jem.

'What d'you mean?' Ned protested. 'I won.'

'Nah, you picked the hand with the bit of wood in it,' said Jem. 'That means you lost.'

66

Captain had never had a warm relationship with cats. The only ones he had known were the feral moggies that scoured the streets for food, fighting viciously over every scrap. They would arch their backs and swear at him if he went anywhere near them and clawed his hands if he tried to stroke them. But the little grey cat crouching on the ledge, its body convulsed by shock, was not wild. From its fat stomach and abundant fur, plastered against its body now, Captain could tell it was somebody's beloved pet that had, like many others, found its way into the sewers, never to get out again.

'Want to come with me?' he said, reaching for it cautiously.

The cat gave a nervous miaow and backed away from him, flattening itself against the wall.

'It's all right,' Captain said, trying to sound encouraging. 'I'm not goin' to hurt you. Honest,

I'm not. What's your name? I'll bet it's somethin' soft like Pussy or Kitty. Well, I'm not havin' no cat with a sappy name like that. I know, Mother Bailey used to have a cat just like you. What was his name? Maurice. Like that name, do you? Good. Come on, Maurice.'

And picking up the cat, he put it in his tosher's bag.

67

'There is no child by the name of Clara Forbes in this house. How many more times must I say it?'

'But I was told—'

'By whom, may I ask?' The clerk peered at Clara's mother over his glasses. It was quite obvious that he did not approve of her or her ragged clothes, and the woman shrank from his disdainful expression.

'By a crossin' sweeper in the Square,' she mumbled, staring at the floor.

'A crossing sweeper?' The clerk could scarcely believe his ears. 'A crossing sweeper? Are you saying that you believe the word of a crossing sweeper over mine?'

'Nah, sir. Sorry, sir.' The woman made to curtsy at the same time as backing away and almost fell. 'I must've got the wrong workhouse or . . . or perhaps the kid that told me got it wrong.'

'Indeed,' said the clerk frostily, snapping the ledger shut. 'Good day to you, madam.'

As soon as Clara's mother had gone, Blood stepped out from behind the cupboard where he had been hiding listening to the conversation.

'Well done, Mr Lloyd.' He went to give the clerk a pat on the back, but his eyes were not focusing too well and he patted the chair instead. Fumbling in his pocket he eventually pulled out a half-crown, which he put on the table.

'Thank you, sir,' said the clerk, closing his hand over it. 'I think I know where my duty lies. There is one problem, however.'

'A problem, Mr Lloyd?' Blood frowned.

'What happens when Polly — I mean, Clara Forbes — eventually leaves here? She will inform her mother that . . .'

'Leaves here, Mr Lloyd?' Blood found that very droll. 'That girl will never leave here. She'll stay in the dead-housh . . . house till she's a corpsh . . . corpse herself. Them boys too,' he added, making a great effort not slur his words again. 'Nah, they're none of them goin' to leave here, Mr Lloyd. Not alive anyway.'

68

One-eyed Eric was sitting in his usual place looking anxiously at the rain as it lashed the walls in squally gusts when Pa strode in.

'Bert!' he cried, trying to rise from his seat. 'Bert the Beast! Long time no see, my old mate. How are you?'

'Better than you, by the looks of it,' said Pa, nodding at the man's shattered legs.

'Yeh, more's the pity. But what brings you here, Bert?'

'I need your help.'

'Lor', I'm popular today.' One-eyed Eric chuckled. 'Everyone wants my help. What can I do for you?'

69

After a while the cat stopped shivering, closed its eyes and snuggled down in Captain's bag. The weight of its body against his ribs comforted him, he was no longer alone, and he chatted to it as he walked along.

'Not long now, Maurice, we're nearly there . . . Maybe we'll get you a nice bit of haddock and a dish of milk . . . Nah, I'm only kiddin'. There's no grub in the workhouse, not for nobody, except the master and his missus, greedy varmints. I reckon Jem, Ned and Billy'll be hungry, I reckon they'd be happy to eat the grub Mother Bailey dishes out. Turned his nose up at it, he did, that Jem. Oh yeh, it wasn't good enough for the likes of him. I'll wager he'd scorf a bowlful of Mother Bailey's gruel now . . . And so would I,' he added as his stomach rumbled. 'I don't know how I'm goin' to get in the workhouse, Maurice, straight I don't. Climb up the ladder, open the cover and see what happens, I suppose. Leave it to fate, as One-eyed Eric's missus always used to say. Not that it did her much good.' He frowned. 'You all right in there, Maurice?' He lifted the bag and peered in. The cat was fast asleep. 'Havin' a bit of a nap, are you? That's the ticket! Wish I could get in there with you and have a nap myself.' Captain laughed. And the sound of his laughter lifted his spirits.

 297

70

Muttering and cursing, Ned began to climb up the coffins.

'It's very wobbly,' he said.

'Nah, it's safe as houses,' said Jem.

'I'm goin' to fall.'

'Don't worry, Clara'll catch you.'

'It's nothin' to laugh about,' Clara scolded him. 'Ned could hurt himself real bad.'

'Nah, he's all right. Look, he's got to the top. What's it like up there, Ned?'

'There are lots of cobwebs and . . . Oh, crikey, I think I just swallowed one.'

'Should've kept your trap shut,' said Jem sympathetically.

'It's not goin' to be easy gettin' these pesky tiles out,' said Ned, tugging at one with both hands. 'I got to pull and pull and . . . Watch out!' he cried as half a dozen suddenly worked loose and fell to the floor. 'Oh well, I done it,' he said, looking at the gaping hole.

'Yeh, you done my nut too,' complained Jem, rubbing his head. 'Well, go on, get out!'

Putting an elbow on each side of the hole, Ned pulled himself on to the roof.

'All serene,' he whispered to the three waiting below. 'Nobody around.'

'All right, Clara, you go up next with Billy,' said Jem, and soon they were all on the roof, lying flat on their stomachs, peering over the edge at the darkened courtyard.

'It's fun up here,' cried Billy excitedly. 'It's like when I went up that chimney at the Oil of Clarendon's and got on the roof and—'

'Stall your mug!' Jem hissed at the little boy. 'If anyone hears us we're done for.'

'There's lights on over there, by the gate,' said Clara, nodding at the receiving ward and the porter's lodge, where lanterns and candles glowed. 'We can't get out that way.'

'What're we goin' to do, Jem?' said Ned.

'Well, I reckon we should . . . er . . . slide down that drainpipe and get into the yard and . . . er . . . and . . . er . . .'

'Look!' hissed Clara suddenly. 'Look!'

'What?'

'There!' She pointed at the manhole cover in the middle of the yard. 'It's openin'. There's someone comin' up . . . I can see a head.' The moon obligingly made another fleeting appearance at that moment and Clara cried out before she could stop herself, 'It's . . . Lor', I don't believe it. It's Captain! Captain!' She stood up, waving wildly. 'We're here! We're here!'

The boy looked up, saw Clara and the others and beckoned to them urgently.

'Where we goin'?' said Billy as Jem pulled him to his feet.

'Gettin' out of this place.'

'How?'

'Through the sewers.'

'That's a real jammy idea,' said Clara admiringly. 'Captain's a real sharp cove.'

'Nah, I thought of it myself. In fact, I was just goin' to say, we'll open up that manhole cover and get out through the sewers. I was!' Jem said indignantly as Ned and Clara burst out laughing.

Sliding down the drainpipe wasn't quite as easy as Jem had thought, mainly because Billy refused to attempt it.

'It's only a little way down,' Jem said. 'So even if you fall you won't break much.'

But Billy would not be persuaded. Squeezing his eyes tightly shut and opening his mouth as wide as it would go, he drew in his breath and prepared to give an ear-shattering bellow when Jem whispered in his ear, 'See that bag Captain's got?' He pointed to the boy who was half out of the manhole, waving to them frantically. 'I reckon it's full of grub he's brought for us to scorf, some of that lovely grub Mother Bailey makes. Ned, Clara and me'll let you have our share if you—' But before he could finish, Billy had already slid down the drainpipe and was running across the courtyard, his eyes glued to the bulging bag around Captain's neck.

71

It had been a disastrous day for Blood and he mulled it over in his mind, growing angrier by the minute: his wife had suffered a gross indignity to her person at the hands of an insolent minx, he and his son had been humiliated in front of a load of stuck-up toffs by a cocky little toerag and he had drowned his sorrows so deeply in porter, wine and gin that his tongue tasted like the bottom of a parrot's cage.

He lurched out of the receiving ward, colliding with the doorpost.

'Damn you!' he shouted, punching it so hard he almost broke his fingers.

The clerk glanced up and quickly lowered his eyes again. Blood was a volatile, violent man and it was wiser to say and do nothing when he was in one of his drunken rages.

The master stood in the doorway nursing his bruised hand. The pain made his temper even worse and he turned to the clerk, who was writing in his ledger with a quill pen, and snapped, 'That pen makes the very devil of a row, Mr Lloyd.'

'Sorry, sir,' said the clerk, putting it down.

'Well, don't stop!' Blood reprimanded him. 'You're paid to work, you lazy varmint.'

'Sorry, sir,' said the clerk, picking it up.

'Sharpen it, man! Sharpen it!' Blood's voice rose shrilly.

'Yes, sir. Of course, sir,' said the clerk, opening a drawer in his desk and taking out a penknife.

Frustrated that he could not goad his submissive clerk into some semblance of anger, Blood searched for something or someone else on whom to vent his spleen . . . Four little faces suddenly popped into his head, four infuriating children, four difficult, disobedient, defiant urchins who were the cause of all his misfortunes that day.

He had been too easy on them, their punishment had been too lenient. True they would die of starvation eventually but in the meantime they were sleeping contentedly in the dead-house. No! Blood raised his fist to strike the doorpost again but stopped himself in time. No, they had to be thrashed, soundly thrashed, all of them, even the little one — he was as bad as his brothers, a mischievous little cub, creating mayhem in the infants' ward ...

Blood grabbed the lamp from the clerk's desk, leaving him in darkness, and staggered over to the carpenter's shop. As luck would have it the men had been making broom handles, long, thick poles that would not break or splinter under pressure.

Blood chose the longest and thickest, beaming ghoulishly at the thought of the pain it would inflict on bare buttocks, and set off for the dead-house.

Out of the corner of his eye he suddenly saw – or thought he saw – a figure, a shape, perhaps an animal, run across the far end of the yard and disappear as if the ground had swallowed it up.

'W-what?' He passed a trembling hand over his eyes.

Something else dashed across and disappeared.

'Oh, Lor'!' He broke into a cold sweat – was he going mad? Was the gin and porter rotting his brain? He knew of men and women, heavy drinkers, incurable alcoholics, who wandered the streets seeing demons, shouting at phantom figures, until they were dragged away to a lunatic asylum.

A third shape sped across the yard, crouching low. Then a fourth.

Blood held up the lamp. The light it gave was not strong. Nevertheless it was sufficient for him to make out Jem's head framed by the manhole cover. The next moment it sank out of sight and the cover was pulled shut.

It took a moment or two for Blood's befuddled brain to comprehend what had happened. He stood, rocking back and forth, staring at the cover, his mouth opening and closing. At last, with the force of a train slamming into the buffers at high speed, the realization hit him – the brats had escaped!

Bellowing a string of oaths and threats at the top of his lungs he charged down the courtyard, brandishing the broom handle like a lance.

'What's up with Blood?' cried the porter, running out of his lodge.

The clerk raised his hand to his mouth in a pouring motion.

'Oh.' The porter gave a knowing nod. 'Seein' pink spiders again, is he? If he doesn't give up the booze he'll go barmy.'

'I rather think he already has,' said the clerk drily, watching Blood tear open the manhole cover and scream into the gaping hole.

'Nothin' we can do about it, Mr Lloyd. We'd best

leave him to it,' said the porter, going back into his lodge. 'He'll sober up. In time.'

'I agree with you, Mr Buxted,' said the clerk. And in the absence of a lamp to work by he closed the door of the receiving ward and went home.

72

'Follow me close,' said Captain as the children climbed down the ladder into the murky sewers. 'Slide your feet along the bottom, only go where I go and don't touch nothin'.' And swinging Billy on to his shoulders he set off with Clara next, the filthy water up to her thighs, followed by Jem and Ned.

'I c-c-can't see nothin',' whispered Ned, fear making his voice shake. 'I c-can't . . . Oh Lor'!' he cried as he stumbled over a submerged brick and almost fell headlong.

'Put your paw on my shoulders,' said Jem, 'and hold tight. Nah, not that tight, you stupe, you're near strangulatin' me.'

'Ouch!' whimpered Billy, rubbing his head.

'Keep down, nipper!' snapped Captain. 'Them bricks are so rotten they'll fall on us if your noggin scrapes them.'

Captain went on again, moving as fast as he

dared, prodding the floor of the sewer with the pole to make sure it was safe to walk on.

'Captain,' Billy bent down and whispered in the boy's ear, 'I want somethin' to eat.'

'So do I. But we got to get out of here first – *if* we get out.'

'But couldn't I have some of the grub in your bag? Just a bit?' pleaded Billy.

'Grub? I got no grub in here.'

'But Jem promised me. Jem said you'd got grub in that bag and—'

'Don't be daft. All I got is a cat.'

Billy had never eaten cat, but he was prepared to give it a try. 'All right,' he said. 'But you got to cook it first.'

'I will not!' exclaimed Captain in disgust, looking anxiously at the bag in case Maurice had overheard.

73

By the time Ma got to the workhouse the door was shut and locked for the night.

'It's no use, missus,' said an old man watching her as she hammered on it. 'They won't let you in now. You're too late. Very strict about closin' time, the master is. Won't let no one in after nine o'clock, not even if they're dyin'. Well —' he sighed — ''specially not if they're dyin'.'

'I don't want to *stay* in this pesky place,' retorted Ma, shuddering at the thought. 'I want to get my boys out.' And she renewed the attack on the door with fists and feet, shouting, 'Let me in! Let me in!' at the top of her lungs.

After a few moments the bolts were drawn back and the door opened to reveal a very large, very angry porter.

'Pack off there!' he said sternly.

'I won't pack off,' said Ma, 'not till I got my boys.'

'Well, you're not gettin' them tonight. We're

closed for business. Now hook it or I'll call the crushers.'

But before he could slam the door shut Ma put her boot in it, wedging it open.

'Remove that,' said the porter sternly.

'Nah, I won't. Not till I get my boys.'

'Come back in the mornin'.'

'I want them now.'

'I'm tellin' you, missus—'

'And I'm tellin' you.'

'Right, I've had enough of this,' said the porter and he reached out to grab Ma.

Now if he thought she was a weak little woman he could pick up and hurl into the street – as he had so many others before her – he was mistaken. Small she was and often quite sickly for want of decent food and drink, but what she lacked in physique she more than made up for in spirit. No one was going to stop her rescuing her boys that night, not Queen Victoria herself, and certainly not a workhouse porter with the body of an ox and the brain of a gnat.

As he lunged she dropped to her knees and curled into a ball so that he stumbled over her and fell headlong down the steps, landing on the pavement with a grunt of astonishment.

'That's the ticket, missus,' cackled the old man, who had watched the incident with glee. 'It's about time someone gave that great tub of lard his come-uppance,' he said, giving the stricken porter a kick in the ribs just for the hell of it.

Ma slipped round the door of the workhouse, locked and bolted it and stood looking about her. There were lights in the windows of the upper floors — dimly flickering candles in the paupers' wards, brightly burning oil lamps in the master's apartment — but the courtyard was in darkness, save for the candle in the porter's lodge which at that moment guttered and died.

'Oh drat, now what do I do?' groaned Ma, for she had never been in a workhouse before and had no idea where to look for her sons. Quickly she ran from one ramshackle building to the next, banging on the door of the bath house, the fever shed, the dead-house and the carpenters' and tinkers' work-shops crying, 'You in there, Jem? Ned, can you hear me? Billy, it's me, your ma—'

'Oy!' shouted an orderly, poking her head out of an upstairs window. 'What're you doin' down there? You should be in your ward.'

'Nah, I don't live here, missus,' Ma shouted back.

'Then you shouldn't be here. We don't take no

one in this late. Porter!' called the orderly, leaning out of the window. 'Porter, chuck this woman out!'

'The porter's not here,' said Ma.

'What d'you mean? Roger's always there.'

'Nah, he's been taken poorly.'

'How d'you know?'

'Cos . . . cos I'm his missus. That's what I've come to tell the master. Roger won't be back for a bit.'

'Taken poorly, is he? Lushy, more like, knowin' him,' sneered the orderly. 'The master won't be best pleased.'

'Where can I find him?'

'He normally does his rounds now, but his missus'll be in their parlour. Up them stairs –' the orderly pointed – 'first door on the right.'

'Thanks, lovey,' said Ma. But just as she was about to climb the stairs the door of the workhouse began to reverberate to thunderous blows and an irate voice bellowed, 'Let me in! Let me in, d'you hear?'

'Who the devil's that?' frowned the orderly.

'I demand to be let in! I'm the porter!'

'The porter?' The orderly narrowed her eyes at Ma. 'But you said he was—'

'It's a looney tic,' said Ma, tapping her forehead. 'I saw him when I came in. He's tellin' everybody

312

he's the porter. Should be locked up, if you ask me. People like that are dangerous.'

'Yeh, you're right,' agreed the orderly. 'We've got enough of them in here already. The sooner the crushers collar him the better.'

And she slammed her window shut.

74

No child under the age of twelve was allowed to leave the workhouse without the permission of a parent or guardian. That was the law and Blood wasn't about to let anyone break it, least of all the Perkinski brothers and Clara who had caused him so much trouble.

Lifting the manhole cover, he hurled it to one side with an oath and lowered himself into the sewer. But in his haste he lost his footing on the slimy rungs of the ladder and fell into the water, swallowing a copious amount before staggering to his feet. For a while he bent over, vomiting the disgusting contents of his stomach. Wisely, for although he was a cruel man he was by no means stupid, he had managed to hold the lamp aloft so that the flame still flickered brightly, but he had lost the broom handle. Bending down he plunged his arm up to the elbow in the liquid excrement and groped around until he found it.

The unexpected ducking in the chill water had helped clear his head and he knew that despite his desperation to get his hands on the runaways he had to tread carefully, testing the floor of the sewer with the broom handle before moving on. Nevertheless he moved much faster than the children and though they did not know it he was closing in on them.

75

The wives of the Board of Guardians sat in the master's parlour sipping from finest crystal glasses and nibbling dainty morsels with gloved hands. They had all heard that something untoward had happened to Mrs Blood but none was quite sure what it was. It wasn't so much sympathy that had prised them from their homes so late as curiosity.

Mrs Blood was tastefully attired for the occasion in a white muslin dress with a boned bodice that dipped to a V at the waist and a full skirt patterned with tiny flowers in pink and lilac. But it was her bonnet that attracted admiring comments from her guests, a pretty confection of green silk taffeta tied under her chins with long silk ribbons.

'Too kind, too kind,' she simpered, coyly acknowledging the fulsome compliments. 'My milliner . . .' She repeated the word in a louder voice in case any of the ladies had missed it. '*My milliner* says feathers are quite the go now. Even Her Majesty wears feathers,' she said, fingering the colourful plumes that some poor bird had unwillingly donated to adorn the back and sides of her bonnet.

'I was most perturbed to hear of your unfortunate contretemps this morning, Mrs Blood,' said Mrs Barrington-Smyth after a suitable interval. As the wife of a banker who was the most important member of the Board of Guardians she naturally assumed the role of chief inquisitor. 'I understand that it had something to do with –' she hesitated, pondering how to express herself in a way that would not appear indelicate – 'with a garment.'

'Indeed it did, ma'am,' said Mrs Blood.

'An undergarment?'

'Just so.'

'How far under?'

Mrs Blood tried in vain to blush. 'Quite far,' she murmured, lowering her eyes to indicate the depth of her embarrassment. 'Can I offer you a soupçon more of punch, ma'am?' she said, glancing at the other ladies to see if they'd noticed she'd spoken French.

'Uhm . . .' The banker's wife hesitated, wondering if it was quite proper to be drinking punch, and so late. Then again, it was probably all fruit – despite

 317

the strong taste of alcohol — so her husband could hardly disapprove. 'Just a little, thank you,' she said.

'Elsie!' Mrs Blood hissed at the orderly hovering behind her chair. 'Wake up, girl! Serve the lady.'

'It is quite delicious, Mrs Blood. And so refreshing,' said Mrs Barrington-Smyth. 'Is it to your own recipe?'

'It is, ma'am.'

'I detect the taste of strawberries . . . and perhaps a hint of loganberries. Am I right?'

'You are, ma'am. It's a very fruitful punch,' said Mrs Blood.

'I don't wish to appear intrusive, my dear lady,' said the banker's wife, returning to the attack, 'but did the mishap this morning occur with your petticoat?'

The other ladies leaned forward eagerly to hear Mrs Blood's reply.

She shook her head.

'Your chemise then?'

Again she shook her head.

The ladies let out a collective sigh and sat back perplexed and not a little exasperated. If one of them did not take this mealy-mouthed bull by the horns, their expressions said, they would be there all night.

'More punch?' said Mrs Blood. 'Elsie, the bowl's half empty,' she whispered in an aside to the orderly. 'Go and fill it up, girl, and be quick about it.'

'Was the garment in question of a more *substantial* nature?' said Mrs Worthington-Fry, whose husband ran a very smart haberdashery in Kensington and therefore felt she had every right to take her place as deputy inquisitor.

'It was,' Mrs Blood agreed.

'Ah!' The ladies nodded at each other, satisfied at last. So it was her corset.

'Laced rather too tightly, I imagine?'

'Much too tight, ma'am,' said Mrs Blood. 'It near done me in.'

'How perfectly dreadful.'

'It was a new girl that done it,' said Mrs Blood. Now that the truth was out, and none of the ladies had had an attack of the vapours as a result, she felt free to give them the details they were longing to hear. 'The little brat . . . the little minx put her boot in my back . . .'

There was a gasp of horror and much fluttering of fans.

'. . . and pulled so hard I thought I'd croak . . . er . . . expire.'

'It must have been extremely painful,' said Mrs Worthington-Fry.

'Oh, it was, ma'am. It hurt somethin' awful.'

'Servants!' exclaimed the banker's wife. 'They are such a problem.'

'So difficult to find a good one,' said the haberdasher's wife as the other ladies nodded agreement.

'They are all lying, thieving . . .'

'And ungrateful.'

'And their language!'

'Quite appalling. I cannot tell you the number of maids I have released from my service for their use of words that are more fit for the gutter than a lady's boudoir.'

'And quite right too,' agreed the others.

'One has to be strict with servants. I trust you are strict with yours, Mrs Blood?'

'Oh, I am, ma'am, very.'

'And this girl has been suitably punished for her misdemeanour?'

'Oh yes, ma'am, Mr Blood's goin' to . . . What the devil . . . ?' She turned round, startled, as the door burst open and a woman stood there staring wildly round the room.

'Which one of you's Blood's missus?' the woman demanded.

The wives of the Board of Guardians stared at her aghast. Not that they were unaccustomed to seeing women with dirty faces and ragged clothes – the streets were full of them – but in the master's parlour?

'Well, come on then,' she snapped. 'Don't sit there like a load of stuffed hens. I said, which one of you's . . . ?'

'I am Mrs Blood,' said the master's wife stiffly. 'And who might you be?'

'My name's Perkinski, Liza Perkinski, and I've come for my boys Jem, Ned and Billy.'

'Well, you can't have them. Leave the premises at once.'

'I'm not goin' till I've got my boys,' said Ma, standing her ground.

'Elsie –' Mrs Blood turned to the orderly – 'go and get Bill and Fred and tell them there's a woman here what needs throwin' on to the streets where she belongs.'

'Nobody's throwin' me out till I get my boys,' said Ma. 'You give them to me right now or I'll . . . I'll . . .'

'Or you'll what?' sneered Mrs Blood as the other ladies shrank back in horror.

Ma looked round the room, wondering what

she could do to persuade the master's wife that she was not a woman to be trifled with. And then she saw the punchbowl, which the orderly had obligingly refilled to the brim.

'Oh, this looks good,' she chuckled, dipping her finger in it and sucking it. 'Mmm. Oh yeh, it's golopshus. Want to try some, my ducky?' And picking up the bowl, she tipped the punch over Mrs Blood's head.

'Waah!' wailed the woman as a wet strawberry slid down her nose and plopped on to her bosom. 'Waah, look what you've done! You've ruined my bleedin' bonnet.'

76

'We're almost at the main sewer now,' said Captain. 'I can see the turn-off up ahead. It'll be easier goin' then cos it's better than these old ones. There aren't so many holes and the roof's a bit higher and—' He froze, every nerve in his body twanging, as an irate voice boomed down the tunnel.

''Oh, c-c-crimes,' stammered Ned as a whole regiment of centipedes crawled up and down his spine. 'It's B-Blood. He's after us.'

'Get goin', Captain, plaguy quick!' Jem urged him as Blood bellowed a series of oaths that would have frightened the devil himself.

Captain moved as quickly as he could, but with Billy on his shoulders and Clara clutching his hand he made slow progress and by the time they reached the main sewer Blood's threats – the grisly details of exactly what he would do to them when he caught them – rang loudly in his ears.

'He's g-goin' to catch us,' said Ned, glancing fearfully over his shoulder.

'Course he's not,' snapped Jem.

'Ned's right,' said Captain. 'We can't go no faster, not with the littl'uns. He'll catch us before we get to the river and—'

'We can paste him,' said Jem, clenching his fists.

'Nah, he's murderous strong is Blood. He'd paste us, more like.'

'So what're we goin' to do?' said Ned, looking at his brother.

Jem gave it a moment's thought. Then, 'You lot go on,' he said.

'What about you?'

'I'm stayin' here.'

'Stayin' here? You off your chump?'

'We're movin' too slow. Blood'll be here any minute. I got to do somethin' to stop him goin' after you.'

'But you haven't got no lamp. You haven't got no pole. You haven't got no—'

'You can't stay, Jem, you can't,' cried Clara. 'You heard what Captain said – Blood'll kill you.'

'Him?' Jem scoffed, glad that he was standing in the shadows so they couldn't see his hands trembling. 'I can handle him.'

324

'But, Jem—'

'Look, stop argufyin', will you? Get goin', plaguy quick.'

'Nah.' Ned shook his head. 'I'm not goin' without you.'

'You got to.'

'I won't,' said Ned, grabbing his brother's arm and trying to pull him along.

'Pack off!' Jem shouted, pushing him away. 'Go on, Ned, go with Captain or I'll give you such a jacketin' . . . !'

'I don't care. You can wallop me black and blue. I'm stayin' here.'

Jem looked at Ned's face and was surprised by the steely glint in his eye. In that moment he knew that for once he had lost a battle with his brother – and in his heart he was glad.

'Oh, all right,' he said gruffly. 'Captain, wait a tick so's we can get across.' He pointed at one of the branch tunnels on the other side.

'Why we goin' over there?' said Ned.

'To make Blood come after us, so Captain and the littl'uns can get away.'

Captain unhooked the lamp from his belt and held it up as Jem made his way across the fast-flowing water of the main sewer, followed closely by Ned.

'You all right?' Captain called when they had reached the other side.

'Yeh, all serene,' Jem called back. 'You lot get goin'. Go on!' he urged as Blood raged and cursed his way towards them.

Though he was sick at heart at leaving them, Captain knew Jem was right. With Clara struggling to keep up and Billy weighing him down they had no hope of escaping Blood unless Jem and Ned could somehow lure him away.

With a nod to the two boys who were huddled together at the mouth of the tunnel, he grasped Clara's hand and set off towards the river – and safety.

'Want to stay with Jem and Ned,' wailed Billy, struggling to get down.

'You go with Captain,' said Jem.

'Nah!' The little boy burst into tears and beat Captain's shoulders with his small fists.

'None of that, Billy!' Jem shouted at him. 'We'll see you in a kick.'

'Promise?' he cried as Captain bore him away.

'Promise!' said Jem, crossing his fingers behind his back.

'D'you think they'll make it?' said Ned in a small voice.

'Course they will,' said Jem. 'Captain's a leery bloke. Besides, he's got the water behind him. Long as he doesn't fall he'll be out of here fast as ninepence.'

'I c-can see light, Jem,' Ned whispered. 'Blood's comin'. What're we goin' to do?'

'Don't keep askin' me what we're goin' to do,' snapped Jem.

'All right. But what're we goin' to . . . ?'

'Wait till he gets here.'

'Then what?'

Jem was searching his brain for an answer to that when an ape-like figure lumbered into view, his vast bulk seeming to fill the tunnel.

'There he is!' Ned drew in his breath sharply.

'Yeh, and he's got a thunderin' great stick.'

Every so often Blood stopped and threw his head back as if he was a wild animal sniffing the air to follow the scent of its prey. Then he moved on. Closer and closer to where Jem and Ned stood watching, waiting, trembling . . .

★

The workhouse master waded to the end of the tunnel and held up his lamp. Jem and Ned could see him clearly now and they fell back in terror for the man was a horrifying sight, his face and body dripping with filth, his lips drawn back in a snarl, his beady eyes aflame with the lust for blood. He stood for a moment taking stock, then he saw the faint glimmer of Captain's lamp at the far end of the main sewer and with a cry of triumph he made to follow them.

'He's goin' after them,' Ned whispered in Jem's ear. 'How're we goin' to stop him? How . . . ?'

'Get him to come after us, of course,' retorted Jem. And cupping his hands around his mouth he hollered, 'Oy! Blood! We're over here, cocky.'

'*Cocky, cocky, cocky,*' cried the echo.

Blood spun round and lifted his lamp, searching the shadows. He scowled when he saw their faces – Jem's defiant, Ned's taut with fear.

'Come and get us, you half-baked old fogey!' Jem taunted him.

'*Fogey, fogey, fogey,*' jeered the echo.

'He won't come,' shouted Ned, joining in, 'he's too lily-livered.'

Blood loured at them with mounting anger and for one moment it looked as if their ruse had succeeded, but then he turned and looked at the tiny figures in the distance, almost out of the tunnel now – Captain with Billy on his shoulders and Clara at his side – and his expression changed. He wanted all of them – Billy, because he had incited the other children to rebel, Jem and Ned, because they had made a fool of him, but most of all he wanted Clara, because Mrs Blood would never let him forget it if the little girl escaped.

'I'll get them –' he gestured towards Captain's little group with something between a smile and a sneer on his lips – 'then I'll come back and drown you two.' And the sewers echoed to his mocking laughter.

Jem didn't know what to do. Somehow he had to do something, say something that would stop Blood – but what? What would enrage Blood so much that he'd forget Captain and Clara and Billy and . . . ? Yes, yes, he had it! And doing his utmost to overcome his fear he began to chant,

> 'Dirty days hath September
> April, June and November . . .'

The laughter on Blood's face turned abruptly to fury.

'All the rest have thirty-one
Without a blessed ray of sun . . .'

Blood lowered his huge head and swung it from side to side like a bull goaded by the toreador's cloak.

'But if any of them had two and thirty
They'd be just as wet and quite as . . .'

Jem stopped short as a noise like a series of explosions reverberated through the tunnels, followed by a whooshing sound.

'What's that?' gasped Ned, clutching his brother's arm convulsively.

'Don't know,' cried Jem. 'Sounds like the roof's fallin' in.'

'Oh blimey! Now we're done for!'

It was not the roof falling in, dangerous as that would have been, but something even worse – rain. It was as if every black cloud for miles around had converged on London and at a given signal released its watery load in a violent deluge. Within minutes the citizens of the metropolis were drenched right through to their combinations and the streets flooded. Water sloshed down the gutters and poured through the gratings into the sewers. Higher and higher it rose like a tidal wave, carrying a fetid cargo of rubbish in its headlong rush to the Thames.

Blood was old enough and wise enough to know what the noise was. He had lived and worked in London all his life, he had heard the stories of toshers swept away by flash floods, their bodies found bruised and battered in the river. If he had not drunk copious amounts of gin and porter that befuddled his brain he would have turned and run for his life. But in his manic frenzy to get to Jem and Ned, to punish, to kill them, he ignored the danger and brandishing his pole and screaming bloodthirsty threats he hurled himself at the two boys.

At that moment a wall of water slammed into him, sweeping his legs from under him. He floundered, struggling to regain his footing, but the torrent was too powerful and as Jem and Ned watched in horror he was carried away.

With Blood and his lamp gone, the blackness that enveloped Jem and Ned was so impenetrable they could see nothing, not a hand, not a finger, even if it had been just a hair breadth from their face. The darkness entombed them.

'Y-you there, Jem?' said Ned, reaching out.

'Yeh.' Jem clutched his brother's trembling hand. 'Well, Blood's not after us no more, is he? He'll be fish bait by now,' he said, trying his best for Ned's sake to sound unconcerned about their perilous situation, for he could feel the fear coursing through his brother's body, convulsing him. 'Poor old fishes, I say.' He made a poor attempt to laugh. 'I reckon they—'

'Jem, we're never goin' to get out of here, are we?' Ned said in a broken voice. 'We're goin' to die, aren't we?'

'Course we're not. Don't talk giffle-gaffle,' Jem blustered. 'We'll wait till the water's gone down, then we'll make a move.'

'Move? How can we move? We got no lamp. We got no stick. We got no—'

'Doesn't matter.' Jem cut him short. 'We'll go real slow, an inch at a time, so we don't fall. It might take us an hour or two . . .'

'An hour? More like a day . . . more like a week,' Ned said despairingly. 'Besides, we don't know where we're goin'.'

'We do. We go out this tunnel and turn left into . . .'

'If we go out this tunnel and turn left we'll be goin' up another one just like this.'

'Nah, we won't. We'll be goin' down the main sewer.'

'We won't, I tell you. That's the one after.'

'It isn't.'

'It is, Jem. I saw it.'

Jem's heart began to thump heavily against his ribcage. If he was right they would escape, but if Ned was right and they went up the wrong tunnel they would wander further and further into the nightmarish labyrinth until they died of exhaustion or starvation or . . . 'Ouch!' he yelled as something bit his finger.

'W-what?' cried Ned.

'Nothin'.'

'But—'

'It was nothin'. Just an itch.'

The water in the main sewer was beginning to subside now and a new sound filled Jem's ears, a stealthy, rustling sound like hundreds of small furry bodies scurrying towards them, surrounding them. Hundreds of small *hungry* bodies . . .

Rats!

'We'd best make a move before the water goes right down,' said Jem, trying to sound calm. But he clenched his fists, ready to lash out at any rat that tried to take another bite out of him. 'It's movin' faster in the main sewer, so . . .'

'So we'll know which way to go!' cried Ned exultantly. 'That's jammy! Come on plaguy quick.'

'Nah!' Jem pulled him up short. 'We got to go slow. If we don't we'll—'

'Cheese it!' exclaimed Ned, clutching Jem's hand so tightly his fingernails dug into the boy's palm.

'Blood'n Tommy!' Jem cried in pain. 'What's wrong with you, you little . . . ?'

'I think . . . I think it's gettin' lighter, Jem. It is, it's gettin' lighter,' whispered Ned, as a dull glow began to fill the tunnels. 'It's . . . Oh, Lor'! It must be Blood. He's not dead. He's comin' back. He's—'

'Shh!' Jem hissed. 'I can hear somethin'.'

Voices echoed through the tunnels, loud, male voices, shouting.

'It's him,' shuddered Ned. 'It's Blood all right, and a load of other blokes. He's brought all his cronies, Jem. He's brought them pesky orderlies. We can't fight them. We can't. They'll rub us out.'

'Not before I've given them a good anointin',' growled Jem.

The light was getting brighter by the minute, the voices louder.

'They're awful c-close now . . . They're awful—'

'Shut your trap, Ned, I can't hear proper,' Jem rebuked him. 'That voice, it sounds like—'

'Blood! It's Blood!'

'Nah, it isn't. It sounds just like—'

'Jem! Ned! Where are you? Jem? Ned?'

'It's Pa,' cried Jem. 'Pa! Pa!' he yelled, nearly bursting his lungs.

'We're here,' shrieked Ned. 'Pa, we're here.'

'Stay where you are,' an unfamiliar voice shouted back. 'Don't move. We'll come to you.'

The light was all around them now, the bright light from a dozen or more lamps attached to the belts of the toshers wading along with Long Tom at their head and Pa close behind.

'We're here, Pa! We're here!' cried the boys as the toshers reached the junction.

'Jem!' Pa cried when he saw them. 'Ned!' And in his haste to get to them he pushed past Long Tom, stumbled and fell headlong.

A dozen pairs of hands reached down and hauled him upright with many a jest at his expense. It took Pa a moment or two to spit the muck out of his mouth and wipe it from his eyes. Then, moving more cautiously, he waded to where Jem and Ned were waiting and swept them into his arms.

'Lor', Pa,' gasped Jem as his father pressed him

close to his chest in a life-threatening hug, 'you don't arf stink.'

'And you don't smell of roses yourself, son.'

'Is Billy all right, Pa?' said Ned. 'Did he and Clara and Cap—'

'Yeh, yeh, they all got out just in time. Captain's taken Billy back to his paddin' ken. We'll pick him up, then go and find Ma —' Pa's face clouded over — 'though Lor' knows where she is, poor soul.'

77

The door of the workhouse opened and the porter, with many a solicitous word, was carried in and Ma Perkinski, with many a curse, was kicked out.

'Told you you were too late, didn't I?' said the old man, who was still leaning against the wall. 'Very strict about closin' time the master is. He won't let no one in.'

'And I told you I don't *want* to stay in that pesky place,' retorted Ma. 'I just want to get some boys out. I know they're in there, I know it,' she cried, wringing her hands in anguish.

'Why d'you want to get boys out of there?' said the old man, perplexed. 'There're loads of them in London, millions of them, the place is full of the little pests, big'uns, littl'uns, fat'uns, thin'uns – you can take your pick. Myself, I wouldn't bother,' he rumbled on, as Ma shed silent tears. 'You can chuck them all in the river, far as I'm concerned. But if you want boys . . . Well, here come a couple – look as if they've been swimmin' in a cesspit. And the bloke with them doesn't look no better.'

Ma glanced up, rubbed her eyes as if in disbelief, sprang to her feet and rushed up the street, her arms outstretched, crying, 'My darlin's! My little darlin's!'

'Well, I'll be jiggered!' exclaimed the old man, scratching his head. 'There's no accountin' for taste.'

78

It was a happy little family that hurried down to the yard by Hungerford Market that night, where Gran and Kate were waiting anxiously for them. Ma was so relieved to have her boys back again she even forgave Billy bleating that he was starving and only a pork pie would save him from certain death – although Mother Bailey had not been so forgiving when the Perkinskis had gone to fetch him from her lodging house. 'You can have him, the greedy little toerag,' she had said. 'He'd lick the paint off my wall – if it had any on it.'

The following morning Pa loaded the pig and chickens into the caravan and they all set off for Devil's Acre.

'Home, sweet home,' sighed Ma contentedly as Bessie plodded into the yard and drew to a halt next to a large pile of steaming manure. 'Oh, it's so good to be back.'

But Gran was not so pleased.

'Look at my caravan,' she moaned. 'Look at it —
a pile of ashes. What'm I goin' to do? What'm I . . . ?'

She stopped, her rheumy old eyes starting out of
her head as an open carriage appeared, pulled by
two perfectly matched black mares, their coats
polished to a rare sheen, their manes plaited with
satin ribbons. The two underfootmen standing
stiffly to attention at the back looked so alike they
might have been twins — which they probably were,
for matching servants were as highly prized as
matching horses.

A tall, handsome man in the splendid livery of
one of the great houses stepped down and looked
about him in amazement, as if he had fallen asleep
and woken up to find himself on the other side of
the world.

'Lookin' for Buckin'ham Palace?' cackled Gran.

Tipping his head back, the better to look down
his nose at the old woman, the footman said, 'Tut!
Tut!' and turned his attention to Ma.

'Am I addressing Mrs Elizabeth Perkinski?' he
asked haughtily.

'You might be. Then again you might not,'
retorted Ma, while the rest of her family gathered
round, gazing in awe at the man's immaculate blue
jacket with silver trim, knee breeches and softest

340

kid slippers. 'And I haven't done nothin' wrong, if that's what you've come about. Nor has my husband, nor my kids. Anyway, it's none of your business if we pinch a loaf of bread or a chicken now and then,' she added with a toss of her head.

'Your misdemeanours are no concern of mine, madam,' retorted the footman with equal asperity.

'That yours, guv?' said Ned, pointing at the smart carriage.

'Course it isn't, you stupe,' said Jem. 'He's just a flunkey.'

'I am in the service of Miss Lucinda Twine,' said the footman, glowering at Jem.

'Miss who?' said Ma.

'Miss Twine is secretary to the Workhouse Visiting Society. I believe you have had occasion to make her acquaintance.'

'Me? I never heard of her.'

'We have, Ma,' said Jem. 'She's the one I told you about – the toff that was in the classroom when I was pretendin' to read that book, somethin' by a cove called Charlie Dickens. What was it, Ned?'

''*Orrible Twist*,' said Ned.

'Yeh, that's right.'

'So, what's she want with us?' Pa asked suspiciously. 'She's not puttin' our kids back in the workhouse — you can tell her that. If she even tries—'

'Miss Twine was extremely concerned to hear of your recent tribulations,' said the footman.

'Our what?'

'Your unfortunate experiences — the incarceration of your sons in the Strand Workhouse and their subsequent ordeal at the hands of —' the footman looked at the blank faces staring at him and heaved a theatrical sigh — 'and the rotten time they had in the sewers, what with Blood trying to polish them off.'

'You're right there, my ducky.' Ma nodded.

'Miss Twine is gratified to hear that all is well,' continued the footman, clearly mortified at being referred to as Ma's ducky, 'and begs you will accept this gift.'

He snapped his fingers and immediately the two underfootmen staggered up with a large wicker hamper.

'Oh, Lor'!' exclaimed Jem. 'I'll wager it's books. She's goin' to make us learn to read.'

All the Perkinskis backed away, staring at the hamper in horror.

'Is it books, guv?' asked Ned in a faint voice.

'No.' The footman gave another elaborate sigh,

342

as if their ignorance was almost more than he could bear. 'I assure you the hamper contains nothing but sustenance.'

'Well, we don't want none of that – whatever it is,' Pa growled at him.

'It's grub,' said the footman tersely.

'*GRUUUUUUUB?*'

Immediately seven pairs of hands reached out and tore open the lid to reveal a huge ham, a game pie, roast chickens, cold sausages, pork pies, kippers, whelks and winkles, eggs, cheese, pickled onions, cakes, buns, loaves, bullseyes and brandy balls.

'I trust it meets with your approval,' said the footman disapprovingly as the family tucked in with gusto, stuffing their mouths with food till their cheeks bulged and grease dripped down their chins. 'Miss Twine wishes to know if there is anything else you require. She says she would be most happy to oblige.'

Jem stopped gnawing a chicken leg for a moment and thought about it. 'Well,' he said, 'since she's offerin', I'd like a new wideawake. A real crack one, made of straw.'

'And I'd like a catapult,' said Ned. 'A proper one, the kind you can buy in Noah's Ark in Holborn.'

'A pair of white silk stockin's for me. Oh, and a

pair of white boots too, if Miss Whatsername can afford it,' said Kate.

'A neckcloth for me. I hear red and blue's all the fashion now,' said Pa.

'And a best bonnet for me with frills at the back and ribbons to tie under my chin,' said Ma. 'And thank your mistress, guv. It's very kind of her, I'm sure.'

'I will convey your expression of gratitude to Miss Twine,' said the footman, turning to go.

'Here, hold hard,' Gran called after him. 'You haven't asked me what I want yet.'

'And what do you want, madam?'

'A caravan.' The old woman gave him a toothless smile. 'A proper one with wheels and a chimney that works. Well, why not?' she demanded hotly as the rest of the family giggled and nudged each other. 'If you don't ask, you don't get.'

'Ma,' said Ned, when everyone had eaten and drunk their fill, 'd'you think we could take some of this grub to Clara?'

'Clara who?'

'The kid in the workhouse with us. We told you about her.'

344

'Yeh, and could we take some to Captain and the sweepers too?' said Jem.

'Course you can,' said Ma.

'But only a bit,' said Billy anxiously, stuffing a pork pie in each of his pockets and another one down his trousers.

'Where does Clara live?'

'Church Street, with her ma and her brother Pip.'

'Here,' Ma said, making up two parcels of food and giving them to Pa, 'you take it to them, Bert.'

'Nah, we'll do it, Ma,' said Jem.

'Nah, you won't. I'm not lettin' you go nowhere near Seven Dials. I lost you once, I'm not losin' you again. Besides, you got work to do,' she said, shooing the boys out of the yard. 'Off you go, the lot of you.'

79

Captain and the crossing sweepers had never seen so much food before, except in shop windows, and with many a cry of 'Lor', what a blow-out!' and 'Thanks, guv!' they set about demolishing the parcel Ma had sent.

It was only a short walk from the sweepers' lodging house to the one in Church Street where Clara lived and when Pa trudged up the stairs he found her and her mother huddled in a corner of the attic with Pip lying on a pile of rags on the floor.

'It's real kind of you,' said Mrs Forbes, looking in amazement at the food Pa had brought. 'It's real generous. I don't know what to say.'

'Don't say nothin', just scorf it,' Pa laughed. 'Go on, Clara –' he turned to the girl who was scrunched in a corner, her knees under her chin – 'tuck in.' But she shook her head and looked away.

'What's up with her?' he said. 'I never seen nobody turn down grub before.'

'She's got the wiffle-woffles,' said her mother. 'She was all right when she came back, well pleased to see Pip again – she thought he'd been snatched, but the woman she'd left the baby with had only taken him round the block to get a bit of fresh air – but now she just mopes around, face like a fiddle. Says she wants to go back to the workhouse. I ask you!'

'Sounds like she's gone off her nut.' Pa frowned, tapping his forehead. 'Bein' in the workhouse can do that to you. They say you go in normal and come out looney.'

'Nah, she's bright as a button, same as always. But she's got a bee in her bonnet about that place. Won't talk about it – says I wouldn't understand. But I reckon there's someone in there she's worried about. A boy, most like,' she added, giving Pa a knowing look.

'That right, Clara?' Pa knelt down and peered into her face.

A tear trickled down the girl's cheek but she said nothing.

'I've told her, you're not goin' back there, my girl, not over my dead body –' Mrs Forbes was close to tears herself – 'but she'll do herself a mischief if she keeps on like this.'

 347

Pa looked at Clara for a long moment, then he reached out his hand to her.

'I'll take you there, my tulip, if that's what you want.'

'Nah!' Her mother clutched his arm. 'Nah, don't.'

'It's all right, I'll say she's one of my own. They wouldn't dare cross me,' Pa said sternly. 'The minute they hear my name they'll start tremblin'.'

80

There was a new porter at the Strand Workhouse, just as burly but not as surly as his predecessor.

'The master's busy,' he said. 'You can't see him 'less you got a appointment.'

'But I must see him,' said Clara.

'Look, miss, I just told you—'

'Tell him I must see him,' Clara repeated, with a steely look in her eye.

'You'd best do as she says, guv,' sighed Pa, 'else we'll be stood here all day.'

The porter hesitated. 'Oh, very well. What's your name?'

'Bert Perkinski – known to one and all as Bert the Beast,' said Pa, sticking his chest out.

'I was askin' her,' said the porter witheringly.

'Clara Forbes.'

'Wait here,' he said, locking the gate.

Moments later he returned and indicated that Pa and Clara should follow him.

'And remember the master's a busy man, so don't waste his time,' he said, showing them into the parlour. 'Clara Forbes to see you, sir, and . . . er —' he glanced at Pa — 'him.'

The new master of the workhouse was a genial gentleman and he shook Pa's hand most courteously and said, 'What can I do for you, sir?'

'Not me. It's her wants to see you,' said Pa, nodding at Clara, 'though I'm sure I don't know why.'

'Well, young lady,' said the master, bending down, 'are you going to tell me?'

Clara hesitated, suddenly overcome by shyness, but seeing the kindly look in the man's eye she leaned forward, put her hands on his shoulders and whispered urgently in his ear.

'What a splendid idea,' he said, straightening up. 'I only wish I'd thought of it myself.'

Pa watched, mystified, as Clara crossed the room to a small wicker birdcage on a stand, picked it up and carried it to the window.

'Here, let me help you,' said the master, opening the window wide.

Clara set the cage on the ledge, lifted the catch on its door and whispered to the bird inside, 'Go on!'

The skylark looked at her with a wary eye, but made no move to leave its perch.

'Go on!' she urged it.

Cautiously it fluttered to the door of the cage and perched there, its head twitching nervously from side to side, making anxious little 'preeh, preeh' chirrups.

Clara gave it a little nudge with her finger and it swooped across the courtyard from one window ledge to the other until it reached the roof. But still it hesitated, as if unsure whether to fly away or return to the safety of its cage.

'Go on!' Clara shouted to it. 'Go on. You're free! You're free!'

The bird looked about it, its tiny head seeming to swivel full circle as if it was seeing the whole wonderful world for the first time. Then with a fluttering of wings it catapulted up, up into the clear blue sky.

Clara craned out of the window and watched, her eyes shining, as the skylark soared higher and higher, singing its heart out all the way, until it was no bigger than a speck on the face of the sun. Then she closed the window, said, 'Thanks, guv,' to the master and, 'Thanks, mister,' to Pa and skipped away, her heart as light as the skylark's.

81

'You let the birdie go, Pa?' said Billy.

'We did, son,' said Pa. 'We stood and watched it fly right over the rooftops. Lovely sight it was, this little bird flyin' up to the sun, singin' fit to bust cos it was free at last. It's probably still up there, flutterin' around in the sunshine, happy as a . . . well, as a lark.'

But Billy was not so happy.

'Why'd you let it go, Pa?' he wailed. 'Why'd you let it go? You should've brought it back here. Ma could've put it in a pie.'

A Note from the Author

The Strand Workhouse

The Strand Poor Law Union covered five workhouses in London. The one to which Flogger Flynn sent Jem, Ned and Billy was on Cleveland Street, which backed on to Charlotte Street. After 1876 it became a hospital for the Central London Sick Asylums District, and the western end of the building survives to this day as the outpatients' department of Middlesex Hospital.

In 1887 a young writer, James Craven, posing as an unemployed mechanic, stayed at the Keighley Workhouse in Yorkshire, which he called 'a disgrace to any civilized country'. He saw the verse 'Dirty days hath September' scrawled on a newly whitewashed wall.

George Catch

I have loosely based the character of George Blood on George Catch, who became master of the Strand Workhouse, a few years after Jem, Ned and Billy were there. A notorious villain and a great deal worse than I've portrayed him, he was dismissed from three workhouses and finally threw himself under a train.

Dr Joseph Rogers

Called Dr Robson in the book, Joseph Rogers is one of the most famous names in workhouse history. He became visiting doctor to the Strand Workhouse when Catch was master. As caring as Catch was callous, he worked and fought hard for the welfare of the inmates.

Louisa Twining

Miss Louisa Twining (my Lucinda Twine) was the youngest of eight children in the famous tea family. As a young woman she visited London's poor in their wretched hovels off the Strand, where her own family lived, and when one of the old women was forced into the workhouse Louisa tried to visit her. Not surprisingly, the Guardians refused permission. Undeterred, in 1859 Louisa helped set up the Workhouse Visiting Society – a group of doctors, barristers, clergy, members of the aristocracy and wives of politicians – and in her role as secretary saw the inside of many workhouses, including the Strand Union. She became an authority on workhouses and a leading reformer.

Constable Rogers

Constable Ross is based on Constable Rogers who, together with Inspector Field, the chief detective at Scotland Yard, took Charles Dickens on a memorable tour of London's worst Rookeries. Constable Rogers was respected by the people who lived in Seven Dials and he could go where others feared to tread.

Noah's Ark

This toy shop in Holborn was founded in 1760 by William Hamley, a Cornishman. In 1881 he opened a new, larger branch in Regent Street and in 1981 it moved to its present site at 188–96. Hamleys is now the biggest toy shop in the world and has around five million visitors a year.

A Glossary of Victorian Slang and Phrases

Neither Jem, Ned, Billy nor the author made up any of the words or expressions in this book, even the golopshus ones. They were all part of common speech in Victorian times.

Addlepated	Stupid
All-overish	Neither sick nor well
Anointing	Beating up
Argufy	Argue
Beak	Magistrate
Blob	Beg by making up hard-luck stories
Blood'n Tommy!/Hell'n Tommy!	Utter destruction!
Bracelets	Handcuffs
Cadger	Someone who asks or begs for something by imposing on the giver's good nature
Chatterbasket	Chatterbox
Cheese it!	Shut up!
Choker	Clergyman
Circumbendibus	In a roundabout way
Clack	Chatter
Combinations	Vest and long underpants in one garment
Costermonger	Someone who sells produce from a stall
Cove	Man
Crack	Excellent
Crawly mawly	Weak, sickly
Crimes!	Exclamation of dismay
Crusher	Policeman
Crushing	Wonderful

Crusty	Irritable
Doll	Girl
Drumstick	Leg
Dumpish	Miserable
Dunderhead	Stupid person
Fancy	Boxing
Giffle-gaffle	Nonsense
Glump	Sulk
Golopshus	Delicious
Goosecap	Stupid person
Growler	Four-wheeled horse-drawn cab
Hornswoggle	Nonsense, humbug
Jacketing	Beating up
Jammy	Wonderful/lucky/profitable
Jawbreaker	Long word
Kicksy	Irritable
Leery	Clever, artful, sly
'Les see kedo'	Romany spell
Molly grubs	Stomach ache
Mullock	Rubbish
Nob	Wealthy person
Noggin	Head
Obstopolous	Unruly, boisterous
Padding ken	Lodgings
Pan	Mouth
Picking oakum	Unravelling rope
Plaguy	Very
Pure finder	Person who collects dog droppings
Ready	Money
Regular crow	Stroke of luck
Reticule	Small dainty bag

Rumgumptious	*Knowing, wide awake, pert*
Saucebox	*Cheeky rascal*
Scorf	*Eat*
Screw	*Stingy person*
Shaver	*Rascal*
Shindig	*Noise, rumpus, row*
Snaggy	*Irritable*
Snatcher	*Kidnapper*
Soaker	*Drunkard*
Spiffy	*Smartly dressed*
Spoony	*In love*
Squally	*Tearful*
Square	*Good, honest*
Stall your mug!	*Shut your face!*
Sticks a-breakin'	*Forcefully*
Stockdollager	*Punch*
Supper club	*Restaurant, usually with entertainment*
Swag-shop	*Shop that sells a variety of poor-quality items*
Swell	*A person showily dressed, aping the upper classes*
Tripes	*Guts*
Trotters	*Feet*
Up to snuff	*Cunning, clever*
Varmint	*Naughty child/rascal*
Walloper	*Beating*
Whacker	*Lie*
Wideawake	*Hat with a wide brim and shallow crown*
Wiffle-woffles	*Moping*

Also by Bowering Sivers

Jammy Dodgers on the Run

London has never been so splendiferous — or so scarifyin'...

Jem, Ned and Billy are the Jammy Dodgers, three scruffy urchins always up to their eyeballs in scams and swindles. But the troublemaking trio meet their match the night they stray into the sinister slums — and Billy gets nabbed. Can Jem and Ned cook up a plummy plan to rescue their brother? Or has little Billy gone for good?

'A foray into the Victorian underworld of thieves, rogues and child-snatchers . . . gruesome. A great deal of fun'

TES